Boogieban: The Play

Boogieban: The Play

By DC Fidler

DCFidler Publishing

<2017>

Published by DCFidler Publishing
1117 University Avenue, #505
Morgantown, WV 26505
DCFidlerpublishing@gmail.com

Printed in the United States of America
by Lulu Press, Inc.

Cover photos by DC Fidler

This play is entirely a work of fiction.
Any resemblance to actual persons, living or dead, is entirely coincidental.

ISBN: 978-0-692-86930-7
Library of Congress Control Number: 2017906524

Dedication

I dedicate *Boogieban* to my father, Carl Fidler, his brothers, Ike and Hugh Fidler, and my dear friends, RJ, Bobby, Brian, Jeffrey, Jason, Mike, Bob, Allen, James, Dan, and Pierce who returned from the hell of wars, and to my dear friends who did not return, Justin and Craig.

I also dedicate *Boogieban* to the numerous brave soldiers who told their stories to me in airports, bars, and my office.

Acknowledgments

A heartfelt thank you to the following friends, colleagues, and mentors:

- Major RJ Casey for his military consultations and endless encouragement.
- Dr. Hamid Tavakoli and Dr. John Lipkin for military psychiatry consultations.
- Dr. Joel Vogt, Dr. Pamela Sullivan, and Dr. Paul Rashid for details on veterans hospital protocols.
- Scott Snyder and Carol Clay Reid for their early encouragement and for proofing my first rough draft of the play version of Boogieban.
- Travis Teffner, who truly embodied Jason Wynsky in original productions of the play.
- Carol Hatcher and Sandi Constantino-Thompson for enthusiastically and passionately proofing my many revisions.
- Travis Teffner, Ashley Shade, Jonathan Lazzell, Sean Marko, Kevin Marlow, Sam Hatcher, Shea Thompson, Kendall Eby, Kasey Kesner, and Stacey Meeker for encouragement and suggestions in developing dialogue and characters in the play.
- M.T. Pockets Theatre Playwrights Group in Morgantown, West Virginia, and the Matthews Lit Ladies in North Carolina for their support.
- Broadway producer Hal Luftig for his brilliant insight to up the stakes for the character of Lawrence by moving him from the backstory to the forefront.
- Andrew Rubin, who pushed me to expand Boogieban and its storyline to create a screenplay, allowing me to incorporate many film ideas into the play and novel.

• My amazing writing professors at the University of North Carolina at Chapel Hill: Doris Betts, Max Steele, Wallace Kaufman, John Parker, and writers-in-residence professors, James Dickey and Robert Anderson. All I have to do is stroll through the Carolina campus, and your warming and challenging presences stir my soul.

• And to my psychiatry mentor and friend, Dr. Jeff Andresen. I hope you recognize that this play is full of many lessons from discussions we had over the decades, including your stories about Paris Island. Your comments helped immensely with character development and maintaining the arc of the plot.

Boogieban opened on February 2, 2012 at M. T. Pockets Theatre, Morgantown, West Virginia, with the following cast:

LAWRENCE	*Donald Fidler*
JASON	*Travis Teffner*
Producers	*Toni Morris*
	Vicki Trickett
Director	*Ashley Shade*
Stage Manager	*Jonathan Lazzell*
Light Design	*Jonathan Lazzell*
Military Consultations	*Major RJ Casey*
	Jonathan Lazzell

Boogieban opened on June 14, 2016 as a staged reading at The Warehouse Performing Arts Center, Cornelius, North Carolina, with the following cast:

LAWRENCE	*Vito Abate*
JASON	*Travis Teffner*
GWYNETH	*Marla Brown*
CHARLES	*Phil Robertson*
JOSH	*Joseph Antoszyk*
NARRATOR	*Jessica Zingher*
Producer and Director	*Marla Brown*
Stage Manager	*Jessica Zingher*

Boogieban opened on September 2, 2017 as a staged reading at M. T. Pockets Theatre, Morgantown, West Virginia, with the following cast:

LAWRENCE	*John Fallon*
JASON	*Travis Teffner*
GWYNETH	*Cindy Ulrich*
CHARLES	*Steve Brooks*
JOSH	*Josh Brooks*
BARBARA	*Chris Adducchio*
JACQUELINE	*Kayla Hudimac*
NARRATOR & SOLDIER	*Justin Grow*
PRODUCER	*Vickie Trickett*
DIRECTOR	*Travis Teffner*

Characters

LAWRENCE	*Military psychiatrist*
JASON	*Soldier patient*
GWYNETH	*LAWRENCE'S wife*
CHARLES	*LAWRENCE'S boss*
JOSH	*JASON'S soldier friend*
BARBARA	*CHARLES' wife*
JACQUELINE	*LAWRENCE'S daughter*
*SOLDIER	*LAWRENCE'S son*

*Soldier has no lines, appears only in silhouette, and can be played by an actor portraying another character.

Settings

All sets can be minimalist in design with blending from one set to another by changes of lighting. The psychiatrist's office can be stage center. The six other sets, consisting of simple furniture, can be located on platforms or rollers to be moved on and off the stage, or located on side-stage turntables.

- Military psychiatrist's office in Washington, DC in April 2010 - center stage
- Charles and Barbara's back yard in April 2010
- Red-sand, desert-mountain area of Afghanistan in February 2010
- Lawrence and Gwyneth's bedroom in April 2010
- James' bedroom in April 2010
- Clyde's, a Georgetown bar in April 2010
- Afghanistan village house in February 2010

Note: Near the end of the play, the lighting should change to hint at the entire stage being an Afghan village. A backdrop of village houses can rise upstage or be projected onto a screen.

"We know how to send our young to war. We know to welcome them back with parades, garlands, and trumpets. We have never known how to bring home their hearts and souls."

DC Fidler
September 2011

ACT ONE

1. LAWRENCE'S OFFICE

The curtain rises on Lawrence's military psychiatry office at Walter Reed Military Hospital in Washington DC in April 2010.
   Surreal spots of light dot the stage. The fourth wall is an imaginary bookshelf. Four books sit on the edge of the stage: Freakonomics, Collapse, The Little Prince, and Textbook of Military Psychiatry.
   LAWRENCE walks among pools of light, talking into a handheld recorder.

LAWRENCE: One model of *Peacemaker,* my family's sailboat. One couch draped with an Oriental rug, like Freud's legendary Vienna office. One small Middle Eastern straw basket, holding rocks from various world beaches. One-thousand-five-hundred-eighty-two books. Thomas Sewall's 1837 *Examination of Phrenology.* A 1938 first edition: *The 500 Hats of Bartholomew Cubbins.* An autographed copy—to me personally: Pat Conroy's *Lords of Discipline.* James Joyce's *Ulysses—massive* book—one day I may read it. Take away my model sailboat, my couch, my rocks, my books. And you have a military dungeon: desk, lamp, three chairs, pile of forms. In this room soldiers talk. People they miss, abusive officers, Dear John letters, what an ungrateful world owes them, who they would have been had dreams been realized.
   (Pause.)
Soldiers by their sides. Sharing dangers of being mutilated or killed. Protecting one another. Oh, they talk about such in mess halls, in the field. But in this office. *This office.* They move beyond. Confide about *threats* to their souls, losing *beliefs* they held as children: what is good, what is right. *Fear*—people back home will never love who they have become, who their country demanded they become.

1

(Pause.)
Tales of loyalty, tales of sacrifice, tales of unsurpassed bonding and intimacy. In actuality, tales transcending love stories, proven by addictive yearning to return time and time again to the brotherhood. Leave lovers, families, friends—abandoned and perplexed.
(Picks up book from edge of stage.)
Of course, soldiers' emotions are explained away. *Textbook of Military Psychiatry.* "Soldiers are expensive resources. Individual soldiers' interests may be sacrificed to further military goals."
(Sets book in box.)
Today, I begin packing for retirement. My books. Store them in our attic until one day they descend to our basement, mold and fade. Two millennia ago, temple snakes slithered along marble floors, Asclepian priests interpreting dreams of Greek warriors. *Those* sacred ruins, sit at the foot of Acropolis, whereas my office, this space I transformed into a . . . a sacred—

CHARLES: *(Interrupts as he pushes open the not-fully-closed door.)* Lawrence! I've got a box.
(Turns on lights.)

(Lights change to normal office setting.)

CHARLES: What the hell are you doing in the dark?

LAWRENCE: Dictating memoirs. I think better in the dark.

CHARLES: Memoirs? On tape? Who even still sells tapes?

LAWRENCE: I saved a crate of them.

CHARLES: God, you're stubborn. And you're late.

LAWRENCE: You know I hate parties.

CHARLES: You hate parties that honor you. We kept it simple. I appreciate you are retiring, ready to bust the hell out, but Bingham's got pneumonia. I need you to see one more patient.

LAWRENCE: You complicated my life in Vietnam and every moment since.

CHARLES: Thirty-minute evaluation. Simple.

LAWRENCE: Simple? Sure. Why not?

CHARLES: Memoirs. Shit. You aren't going to go out easy, are you, you son of a bitch?
(Exits.)

(LAWRENCE lifts a folded American flag in a display box from shelf and holds it to his chest.)

GWYNETH: *(Appears in doorway.)* Okay if I come in?

LAWRENCE: *(Quickly returns box to shelf.)* I need more packing boxes.

GWYNETH: Donate your books to my psych department.

LAWRENCE: Thirty years of classics?

GWYNETH: How is that going to look? Your books piled all over our house.

LAWRENCE: Did you come here for my retirement party or to cajole me into getting rid of my books?

GWYNETH: At least donate half of them.
(Hands gift to LAWRENCE.)
Jacqueline wants you to have a photo of the three of us.

LAWRENCE: People retiring don't add clutter.

GWYNETH: Give it back.

LAWRENCE: No, no. I'll put it on my desk. Family photos are fine for your office. Your patients are Georgetown faculty members. My patients are damaged, horny soldiers who will lust after my wife and daughter.

GWYNETH: As they should.

(LAWRENCE opens gift, freezing as he looks at two photos in a platinum frame.)

GWYNETH: I also included a photo of James sailing with us on *Peacemaker*.

LAWRENCE: I was not prepared for that. You should have warned me.

GWYNETH: He wore his cadet uniform to impress Megan.

LAWRENCE: He wore it to impress *me*. He didn't invite Megan. You did. And you threw one heck of a fit when he wouldn't pose with her.

GWYNETH: All I asked for was one photo.

LAWRENCE: He didn't want you to assume he and Megan were more than friends.

GWYNETH: I wanted a photo of my handsome son with a beautiful woman.

LAWRENCE: *He* felt it was wrong.

GWYNETH: Jacqueline is thrilled the three of us are sailing together this afternoon. She skipped a sorority meeting to go with us.

LAWRENCE: Charlie asked me to see one-more patient.

GWYNETH: This is the fourth afternoon you canceled on us.

LAWRENCE: Charlie *needs* me to see—

GWYNETH: I know what you're doing. You step foot onto *Peacemaker* and you miss James. You have a beautiful daughter aching to spend time with you. She feels you shun her.

LAWRENCE: Mother and daughter talks.

GWYNETH: You certainly are going to miss your young soldiers.

LAWRENCE: Don't do that! I don't analyze you.

GWYNETH: She'll be grown soon. Ask Charlie not to assign you patients. It's not healthy. He's *had your six* since Vietnam. He'll understand.

LAWRENCE: No, he won't understand. It's too big to understand.

GWYNETH: *(Looks out window.)* Should be splendid sailing. Strong April Northeast winds.

LAWRENCE: I put a new winch handle in the starboard locker. The new boy in the shop said it will make trimming the jib easier.

GWYNETH: Well, at least you care about the jib.
(Exits.)

LAWRENCE: Aren't you staying for—
(Studies photos until CHARLES enters.)

CHARLES: Isn't Gwyneth coming to your retirement party?

LAWRENCE: A change of heart. Evidently.

CHARLES: She marched out looking unglued. Anything Barbara and I can do?

LAWRENCE: Thanks, Charlie. We're healing.

CHARLES: Barbara said she invited Gwynie to a grief group for military wives.

LAWRENCE: You of all people should know better. She'll never agree to that.

CHARLES: Come over tonight. Toss steaks on the grill. Salmon for Gwynie. Simple.

LAWRENCE: I'll check if she's on call.

CHARLES: How is it you are completely retiring and she only went part-time?

LAWRENCE: Ask her.

CHARLES: I'll have Barbara ask her.

LAWRENCE: You're chicken shit.

CHARLES: With our wives? You bet your ass. Everyone's *still* waiting for you in the conference room.
(Exits as phone rings.)

LAWRENCE: *(Answers.)* Yes Marcella . . . I can't remember all these soldiers' names. Which one was Melrose? . . . Bad acne? Oh. Wearing those uh farmer-looking things. Yes, bib overalls. That kid lied he was in combat. When he calls, inform him, "no disability, no benefits."

(The lights go down to black.)

2. LAWRENCE AND GWYNETH'S KITCHEN

JACQUELINE, sitting on a barstool at the kitchen bar, sips a ghastly-green protein shake as she works on her laptop. A large, stuffed-toy giraffe is sitting on a chair.

GWYNETH: *(Enters in a huff.)* Your father spent time on the boat last night, but he can't find time to sail with us.

JACQUELINE: 'Cause then he'd have to talk to us.

GWYNETH: In med school, he vowed, "no more military." We married? Immediately he re-enlisted. Deluded me into believing James could get a gold-standard education in military school, *without* having to serve. *Never, ever* trust the promises of men you date.

JACQUELINE: Like I don't hear that every week of my life.

GWYNETH: You're not upset? You drove forty miles here to go sailing.

(JACQUELINE shrugs.)

GWYNETH: *(Walks to chair and picks up giraffe.)* Why is James' giraffe in the kitchen?

JACQUELINE: I was in his room.

GWYNETH: You know I don't want anything taken out of his room.

JACQUELINE: You turned his room into a museum! What's wrong if I go in there?
(Cries.)

GWYNETH: *(Walks to JACQUELINE and hugs her.)* I'm sorry, baby. Not yet. Okay? . . . You know? He never allowed me to wash that dirty old giraffe. It smells horrible.

JACQUELINE: Like he did.

GWYNETH: Yep. It does smell.
  (Pause.)
  I know what! Let's go sailing! You and me. Just the two of us.

JACQUELINE: Not until Dad agrees to go with us.

GWYNETH: Well golly. I guess I just better learn how to sail all alone . . . You are so much like your father. More than James ever was.

JACQUELINE: Is that supposed to make me feel guilty?

GWYNETH: That's supposed to make you go sailing with me.

(JACQUELINE laughs while still crying and hugs GWYNETH.)

(The lights go down to black.)

3. LAWRENCE'S OFFICE

LAWRENCE is standing, reading chart. JASON enters, wearing khaki cargo shorts, a T-shirt, a dog-tag bracelet on his wrist, and a bandage around his left knee. He stands at attention.

LAWRENCE: "Referred by Captain Kendall. On medical leave from Afghanistan. Surgery for a complicated, penetrating PK gunshot wound to the left knee."

JASON: Yes, sir, my knee is good to go, sir!
(Hands a letter to LAWRENCE.)

LAWRENCE: *(Reads letter, crumples it, and throws it into trash.)* Another damn, obsolete form. Have a seat, Specialist . . .
(Looks at chart.)
Wynsky.

JASON: Yes sir, Lieutenant Colonel.

LAWRENCE: "Difficulty with sleep, not liking to be around people, jumping if there is a sudden, loud noise." Yada yada yada. So, you think you have posttraumatic stress disorder.

JASON: Nightmares, sir.

LAWRENCE: Not PTSD?

JASON: No, sir. Nightmares.

LAWRENCE: Nightmares. Okay. Nightmares about things that really happened or did not really happen?

JASON: Do we have to sit like this? Lieutenant Colonel, sir?

LAWRENCE: What do you suggest?

JASON: Move around.

LAWRENCE: I sit with people, Specialist.

JASON: It's like a principal's office. Two conference chairs.

LAWRENCE: I take it you spent significant time in principals' offices.

JASON: Lucca said you'd be tricky.

LAWRENCE: Who is Lucca?

JASON: Specialist Marino. On medical leave like me. I ain't been here two minutes and you got me sayin' I was a bad kid.

LAWRENCE: Were you a bad kid?

JASON: What's that gotta do with my nightmares?

LAWRENCE: Maybe nothing.

JASON: Or maybe lots. That's what yer thinkin', right? Can I move? Stand, sir? Colonel, sir?

LAWRENCE: Sure. Stand.

JASON: *(Marches to certificate on wall and reads.)* "For wounds received in combat action . . . Republic of Vietnam." Purple Heart.
(Walks to table and picks up photo frame.)
Who are they?

LAWRENCE: My wife and daughter.

JASON: Movie-star lookin' lady. How old's your daughter? Hey! I seen that cadet at Fort Bennin'. Bunch'a guys wuz pokin' fun at'im. Callin'im names.

(LAWRENCE grabs the frame and places it lying face down on desk.)

JASON: *(Picks up the model sailboat.)* Figured you come from wealth.

LAWRENCE: *(Takes sailboat and places it back on stand.)* Why do you think that?

JASON: *(Taps back of photos.)* The clothes.

LAWRENCE: We were attending a family acquaintance's wedding.

JASON: Your black Rolex Submariner.

LAWRENCE: It's an old gift of gratitude from a beholden GI's father.

JASON: The way you talk.

LAWRENCE: Do you come from wealth?

JASON: Are you kiddin'? Shit. First time anybody asked me if I come from wealth. Yer probably makin' fun'a me. I don't have PSTD.

LAWRENCE: PTSD.

JASON: PT . . . That . . . You read all these books?

LAWRENCE: Many. Some I partially read.

JASON: Holy shit this book's old.
(Pulls imagined book from imagined shelf.)

11

(LAWRENCE is alarmed. JASON notices and quickly pushes book back into shelf.)

LAWRENCE: What do you like to read?
(Pause.)
No comment?

JASON: Stephen King.
(Pause.)
No comment?

LAWRENCE: What do you like about Stephen King?

JASON: I don't read no Stephen King.

LAWRENCE: Oh, why did you say that you—

JASON: *Great Expectations.*

LAWRENCE: Who has great expectations?

JASON: It's a book, sir. Charles Dickens. Now you gonna make fun'a me?

LAWRENCE: *Great Expectations* is a fine novel.

JASON: *Cujo* and *The Tommyknockers* are shit?

LAWRENCE: Did you like those Stephen King books?

JASON: I ain't read'em. I'm tricky, too.

LAWRENCE: I see that, Wynsky.

JASON: That piss you off?

LAWRENCE: That you're playful?

JASON: Playful? Hmm. Thought I was impertinent.

LAWRENCE: Ah. A label from the principal's office.

JASON: And a disappointment.

LAWRENCE: Reading *Great Expectations*?

JASON: I was paid to read it. And interpret it.

LAWRENCE: Interpret?

JASON: Wrote a paper. "Summer in the Light and Winter in the Shade."

LAWRENCE: What else were you paid to read? *And* interpret?

JASON: *Oliver Twist. A Tale of Two Cities.* Sixth grade teacher. Miss Buckland.

LAWRENCE: Did you get wealthy being paid to read?

JASON: Five dollars a book.

LAWRENCE: Not much. So, you read classics.

JASON: Goodness gracious. High school dropout's got riches'a the mind cuz he read classics.

LAWRENCE: What was your most recent book?

JASON: *Cujo . . . Freakonomics.* You read it?

LAWRENCE: Partially.

JASON: It's on your partially read bookshelf?

LAWRENCE: It is.

JASON: What was your last book?

LAWRENCE: What do you imagine it was?

JASON: I don't want to imagine. I want you to answer like I answered you.

LAWRENCE: Like you answered me. Okay . . . *Cujo*.

JASON: Not only tricky, but a wise ass.

LAWRENCE: George Bush's Autobiography.

JASON: No shit. I don't picture you likin' that guy. Or wuz it one'a those know-yer-enemy kind'a things? Oops. Crossed the boundary on that. I apologize, Lieutenant Colonel, sir. Sincerely. Obvious I grew up on the wrong side'a the tracks. Lucca said that—

LAWRENCE: You mentioned Lucca earlier.

JASON: Marino. Taliban blew his ankle to hell. Lucca said he heard people who grow up underprivileged, who have shit for childhoods, *them people* get PSTD.

LAWRENCE: PTSD.

JASON: PTSD.

LAWRENCE: Post-traumatic stress—

JASON: I know, I know. Jest my dyslexia pokin' through.

LAWRENCE: Ah! You were diagnosed with dyslexia.

JASON: Shit. Give me a gold medal. I have dyslexia but read *Les Miserable*.

LAWRENCE: Sweet accent. You read it in French?

JASON: Fuckin' snob. Miss D'Amici didn't pay me enough to read it in French.

LAWRENCE: You said Miss Buckingham paid you.

JASON: Miss Buckland. She wuz sixth grade. Miss D'Amici eighth.

LAWRENCE: Why did you drop out? Teachers quit paying you?

JASON: Heather Miles. Got pregnant. Her parents sent her away. Never asked me. I worked a few months. Signed up.

LAWRENCE: An abortion.

(JASON does not respond.)

LAWRENCE: Stirs up feelings.

JASON: Drop it!

(LAWRENCE stands with firm military stance.)

JASON: Please, sir.
(Thumbs through the book Freakonomics.)
You only read three pages of *Freakonomics*?

LAWRENCE: If that's where the bookmark is.

JASON: That don't even count as, "I partially read it." Probably didn't even read the preface. I bet you have a bookmark in each'a these hundreds'a books. Partially read.

LAWRENCE: How much do you want me to read?

JASON: All . . . Oh. Read me? More than fuckin' three pages.

LAWRENCE: How many pages are we up to now?

JASON: The front book cover.

LAWRENCE: Guess I'm not that tricky.

JASON: You're tricky. Scary tricky.

LAWRENCE: Maybe you're scared what we'll find out about you.

JASON: Maybe I'm scared you're scared what you'll find out about me. Why can't we do this in a bar? Over a Sam Adams or a Killian's?

LAWRENCE: Nice beers.

JASON: You think I'm a Bud Light guy? You hurt my feelin's, Doc. President Obama? Our Commander in Chief has the White House brew his brews. Lieutenant Bumbgardner let me drain one.

LAWRENCE: You have connections. How old are you?

JASON: You gonna card me? Shit. I fuckin' risk my life over there, shoot my weapon at the Taliban to make our country secure, but can't sip a brew. One'a my under-aged buddies is layin' in a hospital. Can't speak. Does that make sense?

LAWRENCE: Doesn't make sense to you.

JASON: No. I asked you. Does that make sense to you?

LAWRENCE: Yes.

JASON: As in yes that makes sense?

LAWRENCE: Yes.

JASON: Screw you!

LAWRENCE: The reason people like me send you to war is the same reason I don't want you to drink. Your frontal lobes don't work, turned off by your relentless barrage of youthful sexual hormones.

JASON: What the hell?

LAWRENCE: You make poor decisions, take risks. Mature people's frontal lobes work. We limit our drinking. We sure as hell don't grab weapons and run screaming into tribes of Taliban.

JASON: So, yer sayin' mature people like you take advantage'a us. Send us to fight wars old farts start.

LAWRENCE: Mature farts exploit immature farts.

JASON: Shit. That was damn honest, sir.

LAWRENCE: Wynsky? Scares me what comes out of me sometimes.

JASON: What comes outta you scares *me*.

LAWRENCE: Truth.

JASON: Oh. There you go. Tricky. Fuckin' clever.

LAWRENCE: I studied years to be clever.

JASON: The books you more than partially read?

LAWRENCE: The books I fully read. Took notes. Underlined. So . . . your nightmares.

JASON: Now why did you go and do that? Ruin our friendly time together.

LAWRENCE: You came here to get rid of nightmares.

JASON: I come here 'cause I was *referred*. They're not yer nightmares. They're mine. I own them.

(Office lights go to black. Lights rise on JOSH standing on red-sand set with his weapon. JASON walks to set and picks up a weapon. They cautiously patrol.)

JOSH: *(Suddenly scares JASON by grabbing him and laughing.)* Don't let them *Boogieban* grab you, pretty boy!

JASON: Shit, Josh! The Taliban?

JOSH: Taliban, shit. They ain't people, Wynsky. When you dream? They crawl up outta the sand and carve you.

JASON: I don't believe yer Boogieman crap.

JOSH: *Boogie-ban.* In them rocks, past the dunes. Smell'em? You smell'em cause'a the goat brains they eat. All 'round us skinned goats hangin' in trees. They snatch us. Drag us off like baby goats. One by one. Skin us alive. Shhh. Listen. Hear that? That sound ain't always jest wind.

JASON: What is it?

JOSH: Dalton was layin' on top'a dune, half asleep. They turned their backs five seconds. Never heard nothin'. Gone. Two weeks later, Santiago found a pile of somethin' that hardly looked like Dalton.

18

JASON: Maybe it wuzn't Dalton.

JOSH: His dog tags, Wynsky! . . . Boogieban.

JASON: Shit . . . Boogieban.

(Return to normal office lighting as JASON returns to office.)

LAWRENCE: Where were you just then?

JASON: Oh . . . Sorry, sir. Nowhere.

LAWRENCE: While you were nowhere, I said, "You are the author of your nightmares."

JASON: Oh. I didn't hear you.

LAWRENCE: Well? Do you agree?

JASON: If I agree you'll say my nightmares are fiction. If I disagree you'll say my nightmares are true. Things that really happened. Even with shelves of underlined books, tricks don't work.

LAWRENCE: When two people value truth? That works.

JASON: I ain't read yer books, but I believe brains can't handle truth.

LAWRENCE: Huh. That's what my books say.

JASON: So . . . Yer bein' nice to me. What do you git outta it?

LAWRENCE: Truth.

JASON: When we want truth outta Hadjis we catch, we torture'em.

LAWRENCE: Ignorance!

JASON: Yer a piece of art, Doc. I might jest end up likin' you . . . Aren't you allowed to say you might one day like me, too, or won't like me? See? At a bar, you could say four little words, "I like you Jason."

LAWRENCE: And if I said, "Wynsky, I like you?"

JASON: Shit. That wuz like sayin' it but not sayin' it. Like one'a my girlfriends. "And if I said I liked you?"

LAWRENCE: If we drank beers you'd talk about nightmares?

JASON: Maybe.

LAWRENCE: How many beers?

JASON: Enough we'd have to hold each other up.

(Lights rise on the red-sand set as remain up on office.)

JOSH: *(Drinks from a Mason jar full of clear liquid.)* Middle East. Hell, I don't give a shit. Let's swig down some moonshine, Jace. Arkansas laid his hands on it. It'll put hair on that bald baby peach-fuzz chest you got.

LAWRENCE: Who usually holds you up?

JASON: Change the subject.

LAWRENCE: Three forbidden topics: abortions, who holds you up when you're drunk . . . and nightmares.

JOSH: You scared to try it, Wynsky? Fuckin' fraidy cat.

JASON: *(Joins JOSH as office lights fade.)* Gimme that. *(Grabs jar, drinks, coughs, and spits.)* Damn, Josh! You jest poisoned me.

JOSH: *(Laughs.)* You gotta grow a stomach if yer gonna drink Texas moonshine, boy. Jest like Texas barbecue, it's the best.

JASON: Bullshit. Georgia pit-cooks the tastiest cue.

JOSH: Dream on, redneck.

JASON: Josh? . . . How'd I do this mornin'? On that hill?

JOSH: Khosrow? You wuz there. Why you askin'?

JASON: Jest askin'.

JOSH: You done fuckin' fantastic, buddy. Even Texans'd be proud'a ya.

JASON: Did I shoot anybody?

JOSH: Hell yeah! When I started shootin' over that little wall me and you wuz behind, you took a knee jest like me, positioned yer M16, and sprayed three-round bursts like a crazy fuck. Run screamin' and firin' right at'em. Everybody followed you. We took out them two fuckin' PKs in three minutes flat. Everybody seen it. Everybody's braggin', hollerin', "Wynsky, you the man!"

JASON: I don't remember.

JOSH: Whatever, man. We wuz all takin' on fire . . . Wait a minute, wait a minute. Look at me . . . You honest to gosh don't remember?

JASON: Jest remember gittin' up side'a ya.

JOSH: Maybe . . . cuz you got knocked out a minute.

JASON: I dunno.

JOSH: Look . . . I think it's a blessed gift folks can't remember bad spots they's stuck in. Lots'a mess I wish I could block out.

JASON: But you remember today.

JOSH: Plum remember seein' you go fer'em, yeah. Man, I like seein' that play in my head. Never'll git tired'a seein' that . . . Listen! All you gotta know, buddy, is you done good today, and you better know I'm damn proud'a ya. Got that? And you better be proud'a yerself. All'a us is proud'a ya. Let's grab some more'a that only-half-as-good-as-Texas pizza.

(Lights fade on red-sand set and rise on office as JASON returns to office.)

LAWRENCE: *(Picks up a medicine vial.)* There are medications that can relieve combat nightmares.

JASON: What about ownin' my nightmares do you not fuckin' understand?

LAWRENCE: You have a dog tag on your wrist.

(JASON pulls off his dog-tag bracelet, places it in his pocket.)

LAWRENCE: You have dog tags around your neck.

JASON: That's where we wear our two dog tags. Sir!

LAWRENCE: *Not* on your wrist, Specialist.

JASON: People in your photos: your wife and daughter. Who's the cadet?

LAWRENCE: That's personal.

JASON: Would you lay yer life on the line fer'em?

LAWRENCE: You know I would.

JASON: People say bullshit words: honor, country, duty.

LAWRENCE: Say words but do not live them.

JASON: A blood-thirsty killer breaks into yer home. You can save one. Which one?

LAWRENCE: Why only one?

JASON: EEEH! Times up. Now they're all dead. A Taliban psycho bursts through that door. He's gonna blast his PK in two seconds. You or me? EEEH! Times up. We're both dead. Fuckin' retard.

LAWRENCE: Hey! Let's slow this down.

JASON: It don't slow down.

LAWRENCE: That's the way it is.

JASON: A thousand times faster.

LAWRENCE: That would give anyone nightmares.

JASON: Useless people. "Oh, there was an explosion three miles over the ridge. Poor me. I can't sleep."

LAWRENCE: Worse happens.

JASON: You want me to paint you a fuckin' picture? You ain't earned it, *Lieutenant!*

LAWRENCE: Your words can never make me know, not like you lived it.

JASON: So why gift-wrap fuckin' words fer you? So you can serve them up in one'a yer books? Run down the hall. "Hey Fred? Guess what this kid Jason told me?"
(Grabs chart and holds it in LAWRENCE'S face.)
Or write in my chart. Name, rank, nightmare number one, nightmare number two, PSTD. Recommendations: medications, read more classic books.
(Slams chart onto desktop.)
I know what yer thinkin'. This kid come from an unstable environment. We fuckin' sent him to a shittier environment: hell. He's not thrivin' like my daughter and cadet in my platinum-framed weddin' photo. He should'a been a failed-to-thrive kid at birth. When we finish, he'll be a failed-to-thrive fuckin' PSTD vet on disability.

LAWRENCE: Unfair, soldier.

JASON: You wanna hear unfair? Meet me at The Tombs.

LAWRENCE: The Tombs? The bar?

JASON: *(Yells as exits.)* Seven o'clock!

LAWRENCE:
(Calls on phone.)
Marcella? Have Captain Kendall contact Specialist Wynsky. Add him to my schedule five more afternoons.
(Pause.)
I know, I know. A terrible idea.
(Dictates into handheld recorder.)
Lieutenant Colonel Lawrence Caplan, Wednesday, 21 April 2010.

(The lights go down to black.)

4. CHARLIE AND BARBARA'S BACK YARD

CHARLES and BARBARA are in their backyard preparing a late-evening picnic.

CHARLES: It's a sensitive issue. Be sure you don't bring it up.

BARBARA: Suicide? I'm sure Gwyneth said James was killed in action.

CHARLES: He was.

BARBARA: So how—

CHARLES: He laid his weapon on the ground, pulled off his helmet and vest, stood up, walked into the line of fire. The guy next to him had just been blown apart.

BARBARA: Oh, my goodness.

CHARLES: That kid was always a loner, a bit off.

BARBARA: *(Takes a stand.)* Well, I found him to be a very sweet boy.

CHARLES: You would. Now you know. So, don't step in it.

(LAWRENCE and GWYNETH appear inside the screen door.)

BARBARA: Lawrence! Gwyneth!

GWYNETH: We rang the doorbell.

BARBARA: You know good and well our home is your home.

CHARLES: I was just about to mix Moscow Mules. Give me a hand.

(GWYNETH steps outside as CHARLES partially steps inside and stares back at BARBARA.)

BARBARA: My goodness, it's been five months. I haven't seen you since the uh . . . since at the uh . . .

(CHARLES rolls his eyes, disappears inside.)

BARBARA: You must be excited Lawrence is retiring.

GWYNETH: I'd be excited if he'd sail with us. Doesn't look good when Jacqueline and I are abandoned to sail our family boat alone.

BARBARA: Nonsense. You two are seasoned sailors.

GWYNETH: Lawrence bought a new winch handle. He's a perpetual optimist, dreaming he can repair or correct everything in the world. Naturally, it was the wrong size.

BARBARA: Well, he repairs plenty of broken-down soldiers.

GWYNETH: That's quite the sports car in your drive. Day-glow orange?

BARBARA: My sister's Porsche.

GWYNETH: I didn't know you had a sister.

BARBARA: Charlene? You met her once. Anyway, she and her wife flew to Italy. They didn't want to risk their Porsche in airport parking.

GWYNETH: Her wife?

BARBARA: They drove up to Vermont and married. I thought I told everybody.

GWYNETH: Oh, I doubt I would have forgotten *that*. Not that it's wrong, two women. Just not sure I'd broadcast it.

BARBARA: I guess . . . you're more private.

GWYNETH: That's an interesting bush. Is it new?

BARBARA: April Snow Rhododendron from our garden club. You should join us sometime.

GWYNETH: Me? In a garden club? I even kill mint plants.

BARBARA: Oh dear. Well, Charlie says you grow fantastic research and teaching programs. Your style of gardening I suppose. I better check on the boys. They'll never find the copper mugs.

CHARLES: *(Yells from offstage.)* Barbara!

(The lights go down to black.)

5. LAWRENCE AND GWYNETH'S BEDROOM AT NIGHT

GWYNETH and LAWRENCE remain fairly intoxicated from the picnic.

GWYNETH: You and Charlie certainly overdid it tonight.

LAWRENCE: And you and Barbara didn't?

GWYNETH: We sipped.

LAWRENCE: Uh huh . . . Did the new winch handle help?

GWYNETH: Hmm . . . How old did you say your patient is?

LAWRENCE: I didn't . . . about James' age. In fact, he thinks he saw James at Fort Benning.

GWYNETH: He saw him?

LAWRENCE: He drooled over my "movie-star wife." That's what he labeled you, "movie-star." I told you family photographs were a bad idea.

GWYNETH: You mean great idea.

LAWRENCE: Must have been what I meant. He asked Jacqueline's age.

GWYNETH: Of course, he did.

LAWRENCE: He walked around touching my photos, my books, *my boat.*

GWYNETH: God knows you hate people touching your stuff. "Ooh, ooh, he touched my, ooh."

LAWRENCE: He read *Great Expectations*. Did your patients?

GWYNETH: Please. My patients are Georgetown faculty members. The kids loved when you read it to us.

LAWRENCE: *Great Expectations?*

GWYNETH: Mountain cabin? Ice storm knocked out the power? Three days of Dickens?

LAWRENCE: Every day I lose memories.
(Pause.)
This guy was in combat, bad as it gets. Won't tell me his nightmares.

GWYNETH: Maybe they connect him to something . . . You talked in your sleep again. I'd tell you, but if I analyze you, it's worse than touching your stuff.

LAWRENCE: You can always touch my stuff.
(Pulls GWYNETH to the floor and tickles her.)

GWYNETH: Stop! Stop! You're drunk. Jacqueline's staying over.

LAWRENCE: She can't hear us . . . So, what did I say?

GWYNETH: When?

LAWRENCE: In my sleep.

GWYNETH: Oh, that. "Moses."

LAWRENCE: Moses?

GWYNETH: Moses.

LAWRENCE: Like Old-Testament Moses?

GWYNETH: You said, "Thank you, Moses."

LAWRENCE: I don't know any Moseses . . . Do you realize when we go out with Charlie, you incessantly twirl your hair with your fingers?

GWYNETH: You're drunk.

LAWRENCE: Libidinous twirling.

GWYNETH: Very drunk. You never call me, "Gwynie" anymore. Always, "Gwyneth." So formal.

LAWRENCE: Charlie calls you, "Gwynie."

GWYNETH: He picked it up from you in med school. The way you seduced me
(Baby voice.)
"Gwynie."

LAWRENCE: I seduced you with a formal, rugged, manly voice, "Gwyneth."

GWYNETH: You are losing memories.

LAWRENCE: A manly voice.

GWYNETH: Uh huh.

LAWRENCE: I'm not sleepy.

GWYNETH: Your soldier'll be fine. He can tell his nightmares to someone else.

LAWRENCE: I scheduled him the next five afternoons.

GWYNETH: You what? You whined that Charlie coerced you to evaluate another patient, and you added him five afternoons? When James wanted to go sailing you cleared your afternoons.

(Lights fade to black for several beats and then an extremely bright white spot abruptly shines straight down upon LAWRENCE sleeping.)

LAWRENCE: *(Gasps beneath the covers and abruptly sits up.)* Moses.

GWYNETH: *(Wakes.)* What?

LAWRENCE: I was lying in tall grass, my belly hurting, staring at small rocks in the dark swamp mud. Someone's jungle boots stepped beside me. White and gray scuffs.

GWYNETH: Oh. A dream.

LAWRENCE: *(Pause.)* What were you dreaming?

GWYNETH: Getting knots out of James' shoelaces. Go back to sleep.

(The lights go down to black.)

6. LAWRENCE'S OFFICE

LAWRENCE picks up the book <u>Freakonomics</u> from the edge of the stage and reads.

JASON: *(Wearing PT uniform and sweating, enters, looks at book cover.)* Freakonomics. Cool.
(Pause and then deliberately pouts.)
You didn't meet me at The Tombs.

LAWRENCE: You waited?

JASON: Four hours. Broke my heart.

LAWRENCE: You waited four hours?

JASON: Maybe four and a half. Don't worry about it.

LAWRENCE: You really waited?

JASON: I really . . . did . . . *not* go to The Tombs. Jest torturin' you. Sorry, sir.

LAWRENCE: So, then you cannot know that I went to The Tombs.

JASON: I didn't see . . . Did you? I feel like shit. Sorry, sir.

LAWRENCE: I did . . . *not* go to The Tombs.

JASON: That's mean, sir.

LAWRENCE: Now I feel like . . . you know.

JASON: Shit?

LAWRENCE: Yes.

JASON: What? You can't say "shit?"

LAWRENCE: Shit.

JASON: That's not very loud.

LAWRENCE: *(Yells.)* Shit!

JASON: Whoa! That's too loud, man. Yer guards'll run in and tackle me.

LAWRENCE: It's sound proof.

JASON: *(Yells.)* Shit!

LAWRENCE: Sound proof.

JASON: No shit?

LAWRENCE: No . . . yes.

JASON: That's cool, dude. So I can yell *shit* anytime.

LAWRENCE: Cry, scream.

JASON: I ain't gonna cry, Doc.

LAWRENCE: But you could.

JASON: What if I got violent? How do they know?

LAWRENCE: I push the panic button.
(Nods toward the desk.)

JASON: *(Looks under the desk and finds the panic button.)*
Very cool. So, you worry I'll hurt you?

LAWRENCE: Someone might.

JASON: Oh, someone might. But not me?

(LAWRENCE shakes head.)

JASON: How do you know I won't hurt you?

LAWRENCE: You don't even like making me wait at The Tombs.

JASON: You didn't wait at The Tombs.

LAWRENCE: The way you acted when you thought I did.

JASON: Oh, so yer sayin' I care about ya.

LAWRENCE: You came back.

JASON: 'Cause you stood me up.

LAWRENCE: You said you didn't go.

JASON: Doc? You keep a stiff face, but feelin's blow outta yer face like sand outta a desert twister.

LAWRENCE: I trained to keep a neutral face.

JASON: Right there. Poor actor face. Don't play poker neither.

LAWRENCE: You think you see it on my face.

JASON: And yer voice, too.

LAWRENCE: Who else's face, voice is it important for you to study?

JASON: Uh . . . Lucca . . . Not since we shipped back. His eyes are kind'a dead, not there.

LAWRENCE: What happened to him?

JASON: Oh. We gonna talk about Lucca, which ain't got nothin' to do with me. Uh huh.

LAWRENCE: Worth a try.

JASON: You should more than partially read your books.

LAWRENCE: Tonight.

JASON: Lots'a reading.

LAWRENCE: I read fast.

JASON: You know? Even for a kid with dyslexia I read fast. Maybe I never really had dyslexia. Misdiagnosed. Like PTSD. I got it right that time? PTSD?

LAWRENCE: Bing, bing, bing. Correct. So what are you saying?

JASON: I see guys, women, told they have PTSD. They don't. Misdiagnosed.

LAWRENCE: What's a more accurate diagnosis?

JASON: *(Pause.)* Broken hearts.

LAWRENCE: *(Pause.)* You know? It's okay if you wear that dog tag on your wrist in here . . . It's not your dog tag, is it?

JASON: Do you think I could have a drink of water or somethin'? I jogged over here. Throat.

LAWRENCE: Sure.
(Pours water from pitcher into cup and hands to JASON.)

JASON: *(Rapidly gulps water.)* Thank you.

LAWRENCE: You're very welcome.

JASON: Very?

LAWRENCE: Yes.

JASON: "Very" is not neutral, Doc.

LAWRENCE: You are one-hundred percent correct.

JASON: Thank you . . . *very* much.
(Drinks more and appears anxious, holds stomach in pain.)

LAWRENCE: Are you okay?

JASON: I must'a drank too much'a yer water . . . When yer nice to me? I ain't used to that.

LAWRENCE: From no one?

JASON: Miss Buckland.

LAWRENCE: Sixth grade.

JASON: I had terrible grammar. Lots'a red marks. But on my content? She smiled every time.

LAWRENCE: And Miss D'Amici?

JASON: You remember my teachers' names?

LAWRENCE: I should do what? Be forgetful?

JASON: Mean would help. You'll drive me fuckin' crazy.

LAWRENCE: Mean? . . . You smell like locker-room sweat.

JASON: I can't help it! I jogged over here in the sun, okay?

LAWRENCE: *(Slides chair away from* JASON *and sniffs the air.)* Better? . . . Not far enough.
(Slides chair a bit farther and sniffs.)

JASON: *(Laughs.)* Yeah. Better. Cool.
(Smells his armpits.)
Damn! I do stink. I thought you wuz kiddin'. Sorry, sir.

LAWRENCE: I should move farther away.

JASON: *Wise ass* is not the same as *mean.* Now, Sergeant Reese was *mean.* We had this war dog. You know. Somethin' soft to pet, lick yer face, sleep against ya. Dogs detect meanness in people. Bill Clinton? Our dog?

LAWRENCE: *Bill Clinton* was the name of your dog?

JASON: Bill Clinton could lick himself, sort of a self-blow job.

LAWRENCE: Bill Clinton.

JASON: Sorry. Anyways, Bill Clinton cowered from everybody in our unit. Especially?

LAWRENCE: Sergeant Reese.

JASON: Growled at him. Teeth showin'. Some war dogs had rough lives as pups. But Bill Clinton loved me to death. Anyways, Sergeant Reese bounced his old NCO grandfather's quarter off my bed so it couldn't possibly bounce like it should. Three days in a row. Latrine duty.

LAWRENCE: What did he have against you?

JASON: One time after laps, we sat under a Live Oak. I sat a few feet away. Bill Clinton hid behind me.

LAWRENCE: You didn't sit with his group.

JASON: Do I look like the group type?

LAWRENCE: What about friends?

(Lights rise on red-sand set. Sound of rifle shots. JASON grabs his weapon and lies on his belly next to JOSH. Sand on the top of the dune blows up into the air with some of the shots.)

JOSH: Shit!

JASON: *(Pulls a toy plastic dinosaur from his pocket and whispers to it as combat sounds continue.)* Big Mama's probably tellin' everybody at church she's worried sick about me bein' over here. Me and you know she's lyin'.

JOSH: What the hell you talkin' to, Wynsky?

JASON: Nothin'.

JOSH: What'cha got in yer hand? Somethin' small. Yer dick?

JASON: I ain't holdin' my . . . nothin'.

(Sound of a jet flying over in a sudden fly-by and quickly fading.)

JOSH: Yee haw! Love them fly-bys . . . Let me see.

(JASON opens hand.)

JOSH: A plastic dinosaur?

JASON: T Rex.

JOSH: T Rex? And you talk to it? . . . Let me see him. I ain't gonna hurt'im.

(JASON hands dinosaur to JOSH.)

JOSH: Very cool. How long you had this little fella?

JASON: Since I wuz four. Don't git moon dust all over'im.

JOSH: Shit. Am I the first to hold'im? 'Sides you? . . . Wynsky, look at me . . . When I wuz a kid, I had this knotted sock. Wouldn't let my nanny Lucinda or nobody wash it. Slept with it.

(Sound of machine-gun blast. Shots scatter sand.)

JOSH: Where'd our fuckin' air support go?

(More shots and more sand scatters.)

JOSH: Fuck! . . . So, I took Socks to kindergarten, to church. When tornado clouds come 'round, I held Socks tight, prayed with'im. I ain't never told nobody that but you. Now we both got things we know.

JASON: Socks.

JOSH: T Rex.

(Sound of machine-gun blast and more sand scatters.)

JOSH: Fuck! I got this bastard.
(Jumps up, takes a knee, and fires M16 in three-round bursts over the dune.)

(Return to normal office lighting as JASON returns to office.)

LAWRENCE: Do you still have T Rex?

JASON: I left him with Jah . . .
(Cannot finish word "Josh.")
Yer makin' me feel stupid talkin' 'bout a plastic toy. Can we move on? Sir?

LAWRENCE: Sure. You haven't told me anything about your family.

JASON: I don't tell nobody 'bout family.
(Pause.)
Okay! I climbed outta my mom when she was fourteen. She got into Ecstasy, run off with my sperm-donor father. Left me with my grandmother. So, that's my family. Okay? Satisfied now?

LAWRENCE: How was living with your grandmother?

JASON: Shit . . . Folks called her, "Big Mama." In front'a church people, Big Mama swore on the good book she loved me to death. In her eyes? Pain. She told mom to abort me.
(Pause and then points at the couch.)
Why do you have that thing?

LAWRENCE: Some people talk better lying on a couch.

JASON: I seen that in movies.
(Walks to couch, removes shoes, lies on couch, squirms.)

LAWRENCE: How is it?

JASON: On top'a this ole rug? Like layin' on KP potato sacks. Lumpy.

LAWRENCE: It's not for sleeping. It's for talking.

JASON: I talk too much 'bout stupid shit.

LAWRENCE: You do talk well.

JASON: You have this annoyin' habit of takin' what I say and twistin' it 'round to make it sound nice . . . People on the couch talk with you sittin' way over there?

LAWRENCE: When people lie on the couch, I sit closer.

(JASON turns and sees chair behind him. He motions for LAWRENCE to move and he complies.)

JASON: I can't see you.

LAWRENCE: You can hear my voice.

JASON: Saying, "Uh huh."

LAWRENCE: Uh huh. Then in your mind, you know I'm here.

JASON: Scoot your chair over here.

LAWRENCE: If you can see me, then my *poor-actor* faces may change what you talk about.

JASON: So I can see you outta the side'a my eye.

(LAWRENCE moves his chair a little closer.)

JASON: A little more.

(LAWRENCE moves slightly closer.)

JASON: Jest a . . .

(And closer.)

JASON: That's good, that's good . . . What do people talk about?

LAWRENCE: Matters of the heart. Matters of war. Early on they talk about things they think are not important.

JASON: They *think* are not important.

LAWRENCE: Traffic, parking.

JASON: Traffic and parkin'? Shit. That is unimportant . . . "Wow, Doc. Traffic wuz a bitch today. I was idlin' in my car in front'a the *Washington Post* fer ten minutes cause'a sewer repairs." And then you would say what?

LAWRENCE: Uh . . . What was it like idling?

JASON: I told you. "A bitch."

LAWRENCE: A bitch.

JASON: Never know when some asshole street cleaner'll set off an IED under yer car and blow you up.
(Laughs.)
Settin' off an IED in downtown DC. Yeah, right. And then you'd say what?

LAWRENCE: I'd say something like . . . "Have you seen IEDs set off under cars?"

(Lights turn to surreal colors in office. Sounds of tanks traveling down dirt road and voices of villagers.)

JASON: *(Goes into a trance and hallucinates. He sits on the edge of the couch back with his feet on the rug cover as if riding atop a tank.)* Bags! That Hadji boy has a video camera. Little bastard knows somethin's goin' down. Shit!

(Sound of explosion.)

43

JASON: *(Jumps to the floor, lies on his stomach, protects the back of his head with his hands.)* Get the fuck out, Bags!

(Return to normal office lighting.)

LAWRENCE: Specialist Wynsky?

JASON: Fuck!

(LAWRENCE walks to his desk, places his hand near the panic button.)

JASON: *(Partially comes out of trance and sits up.)* Traffic and parkin'. Shit.

LAWRENCE: Jason?

(JASON breaths deeply to relax and laces shoes.)

LAWRENCE: What just happened?

JASON: *(Still dazed.)* What?

LAWRENCE: You jumped onto the floor and yelled.

JASON: Nothin'.

LAWRENCE: You had a flashback.

JASON: They don't last long . . . What do they talk about?

LAWRENCE: Who?

JASON: People on the couch.

LAWRENCE: Oh . . . people they love, miss. Shattered dreams, what frightens them.

JASON: Sex?

LAWRENCE: Sometimes sex.

JASON: Deep stuff about sex?

LAWRENCE: Erotic dreams, fantasies.

JASON: Fantasies? Like fantasies when they jerk off?

LAWRENCE: Sometimes.

JASON: *(Talks as hurries to his usual chair and finishes lacing shoe.)* That couch is sick. I ain't touchin' that piece'a crap furniture never again. Uh uh. Move back over here. That couch gives me the willies. You gotta hear a lotta strange stuff in here, huh? Do you think about it when you go home? Back to yer platinum-picture home?

LAWRENCE: Do you remember what happened on the couch?

JASON: No. No, sir.

LAWRENCE: Okay then. Same time tomorrow?

JASON: That's it?

LAWRENCE: We meet forty-five minutes.

JASON: Forty-five. Oh . . . Not yesterday.

LAWRENCE: Yesterday, you walked out twenty minutes early.

JASON: Then you owe me twenty minutes!

LAWRENCE: Tomorrow.

JASON: Damn . . . How do you know I won't fuckin' blow out my brains?

LAWRENCE: You didn't check suicidal thoughts on your checklist. Are you having suicidal thoughts?

JASON: Why? So you can stick my ass in the hospital?
(Walks to door and stops.)
Yer not mad at me, are ya?

LAWRENCE: Not mad at you.

JASON: I didn't hurt ya or nothin', did I?

LAWRENCE: During your flashback? No, you didn't hurt me. I'm fine. Have you ever hurt someone during a flashback?

JASON: No, sir.

LAWRENCE: I need to know you'll stay safe, other people will be safe, and that you'll be here tomorrow.

JASON: *(Returns to LAWRENCE.)* You owe me twenty minutes, Doc. We got a pact.
(Extends hand, firmly shakes, and exits.)

LAWRENCE: *(Dictates.)* Lieutenant Colonel Lawrence Caplan, Thursday, 22 April 2010.

CHARLES: *(Enters.)* I need you to sign this retirement form. Sure you want to do this?

LAWRENCE: I promised Gwyneth.

CHARLES: Soldiers are protesting left and right you're leaving. God knows why they want your ugly face. You're hard as hell on'em.

LAWRENCE: When they need it.

CHARLES: What did you do to rattle that last kid?

LAWRENCE: I was *hard* on him.

CHARLES: Best I keep my nose out of it.

(The lights go down to black.)

7. JAMES' BEDROOM AT NIGHT

LAWRENCE walks into James' barely-lit bedroom. James' T-shirt is draped on a chair. LAWRENCE smells the shirt. He carries James' stuffed-toy giraffe to the bed.

LAWRENCE: James? Remember that book you asked me to read? *A Game of Thrones*? I'm reading it.

(Sounds of gunfire. Lights change so there is a spotlight on LAWRENCE as orange, dream-like lights rise on the sand-dune set's backdrop, leaving the dune silhouetted. A SOLDIER, lying on his stomach on the dune, is barely or not-at-all visible in the darkness. A sudden flash of bright light accompanies an explosive sound, revealing the SOLDIER for a flash. The silhouetted SOLDIER crawls to the top of the dune. Gunfire silences.)

LAWRENCE: Don't do this.

(The SOLDIER stands tall, drops his weapon.)

LAWRENCE: You don't have to do this.

(The SOLDIER removes his vest, and then helmet, and drops them.)

LAWRENCE: *(Screams.)* No!

(The soldier drops behind the sand dune as the lights immediately go to black. GWYNETH enters and turns on the lights. Lights rise to normal evening bedroom lighting.)

GWYNETH: What are you doing in James' room?

LAWRENCE: What?

GWYNETH: It's two thirty. Why are you still up?

LAWRENCE: I let him go.

GWYNETH: Let who go?

LAWRENCE: He gets drunk, dissociates, re-lives combat. He had an episode in my office. Brought up suicide. I should have *locked his ass* in the hospital.

GWYNETH: *(Moves the giraffe to its assigned place.)* I warned you not to treat combat soldiers.

LAWRENCE: If I lock him up he won't trust me.

GWYNETH: At least he'll be alive.

LAWRENCE: As a shadow.

GWYNETH: Like you when . . . Nothing.

LAWRENCE: Like me when what? . . . Gwyneth!

GWYNETH: At our wedding . . . you said, "Gwynie, I give you all of me that came back from Vietnam." In November . . . our son's closed casket . . . I walked up front and spoke. His school friends, his teachers, my father, even my receptionist Michael all shared something about James. Not you. You never even cried. Do you know how screwed up that is?

LAWRENCE: Good for you. You stood at the pulpit talking over James' casket like he was some mythological Roman hero, sacrificed in some ancient battle thousands of years ago. Totally detached. You never even spoke his name.

GWYNETH: I was screaming his name inside!

LAWRENCE: I cry inside every time I see a soldier on crutches or unable to make simple change for a dollar.

GWYNETH: Everyone knows you care. We all admire you. You've been honored with every accolade imaginable. I don't understand what you're trying to prove.

LAWRENCE: I'm not trying to prove anything! I'm trying to rescue this soldier, and by God, no one is going to get in my way! I shall save him!

GWYNETH: Listen to yourself.

LAWRENCE: Did you know James asked me to read, *A Game of Thrones*? On the way to the airport, taking him back to school. What'd I do? Told him I was busy.

GWYNETH: This soldier's not James! Let someone else see this kid! Do something or I will.

LAWRENCE: Good Lord, Gwyneth.

GWYNETH: Get Charlie to reassign this case.

LAWRENCE: That's the fuckin' craziest—

GWYNETH: I am not going to lose you to a misfit soldier!

(The cell phone rings.)

LAWRENCE: *(Answers.)* Lieutenant Colonel Caplan . . . You sound drunk . . . Pistol?

GWYNETH: He has a gun?

LAWRENCE: Listen to me. Put on the safety . . . Listen! Carefully lay the pistol on the ground.

GWYNETH: This is so out of control.

50

LAWRENCE: What's gone? The pistol's gone? I don't understand . . . Out of the wire? You're not in Kabul. You're in Washington, DC.

GWYNETH: Out of bounds.

LAWRENCE: Jason? Where are you? . . . What dumpster? Where? . . . Exorcist steps? I know those steps. Near The Tombs. Listen. I'll come to you.

GWYNETH: You'll what?

LAWRENCE: Jason? . . . Jason? . . . Shit.
(Stuffs phone into pocket.)
I gotta go.

GWYNETH: You gave him your cell number?

LAWRENCE: For safety.

GWYNETH: I'm scared. Don't go. Please, don't go.

LAWRENCE: I'll take a couple of MPs from Fort Meyer with me. Jason needs me.

GWYNETH: "Jason?" Does he call you "Lawrence?"

LAWRENCE: I am taking this specialist to the hospital to sober up, clear his mind.

GWYNETH: This psychotic, drunk kid has a gun!

LAWRENCE: He won't shoot me.

GWYNETH: You have scars where bullets ripped out your intestines.

LAWRENCE: I was a soldier in a war. Soldiers shoot soldiers. I'll call you.
(Exits.)

GWYNETH: *(Calls on landline.)* Charlie. Gwyn. Lawrence ran out after his drunk patient who's lying in a dark alley with a loaded gun. Transfer that patient to Ellen or Brock or . . . You're his fuckin' boss, Charlie!
(Abruptly ends call, calls another number. Forces herself to sound calm.)
Hi Lisa. Sorry to bother you so late. I need a favor.

(The lights go down to black.)

8. LIMBO

Single spotlight rises on LAWRENCE wearing a topcoat.

LAWRENCE: Friends are mirrors we choose for ourselves. The soldier lying in bullet-splattered mud beside me becomes my new mirror. His face instructs me whether I am worth a shit, whether I am loveable, whether I am alive or dead . . . In my office, soldier patients pledge desperate solutions. A bullet to the skull, a deadly cocktail of drugs and alcohol, a car swerving into an unyielding tree, a swim too far from shore. For them, those frightening options are glimpses of peace.
(Pause.)
Specialist Jason Paul Wynsky and his loaded pistol wait at the top of dark alley steps. I shall listen, be captivated in his presence, exorcise his demons.
(Pause.)
Long ago, early humans sat around gazelle-smelling fires, aching to ease one another's torments. Laughter, tears, gestures—didn't do a fucking thing. Humankind screamed in revolt and gave birth to words—words we choke on—some words so strong we dare not speak them.
(Pause.)
I don't know how much longer I can continue with my pain . . . I can't swerve into a mighty oak. I can't swim in a shoreless sea. Tonight, Jason? Do me a big fucking favor.

(The lights go down to black.)

(INTERMISSION.)

ACT TWO

9. LAWRENCE'S OFFICE

Surreal pools of light rise. LAWRENCE walks among the pools of light and picks up a book from the edge of the stage.

LAWRENCE: *"The Little Prince:* You become responsible forever for what you tame." The MP and medics carted Jason away like a tranquilized lion cub off to a zoo. He will wake to mind masters taming him. I envy that kid's spirit. Our twenty-first-century, pseudo-leaders occasionally take vapid actions, profess guilt, and then publicly apologize. The sixteenth-century Italian princes Machiavelli described, led with ruthless, violent actions to preserve their values. It's what we require of our soldiers. No apologies. No looking back. Act, move forward, sleep well. God damn sweetened fairy-tale endings and tiptoeing on eggshells to not offend whiners. Greek gods must sit on Olympus bored off their thrones with humankind. Give me lightning bolts, give me half this kid's spirit. Then, maybe, I will have a hint of hubris to fight for my values.
(Pause.)
I packed away my *Textbook of Military Psychiatry.* Now, I add, *The Little Prince.*
(Places book into box.)
Modern moving forward.
(Turns on lights.)

(Return to normal office lighting. JASON, wearing a hospital gown and robe, eating a banana, enters.)

LAWRENCE: Nurses report you slept less than three hours.

JASON: Sleep sucks in prison.

LAWRENCE: Dr. Jaynes will assess you for flashbacks and dangerousness.

JASON: I am not suicidal, I am not drunk, I am not in withdrawal, I will not drink when I leave, I will not play with guns or sharp objects—

LAWRENCE: You learned hospital speak fast.

JASON: Can I get the fuck outta here today, Doc? Sir? Colonel, sir?

LAWRENCE: We found you passed out at the top of the Exorcist steps. There was no pistol.

JASON: Why the fuck would I have a pistol?

LAWRENCE: On the phone, you said you had a pistol. Was the pistol real or a flashback?

JASON: I called you? *You* fuckin' had me locked up.

LAWRENCE: Your dog-tag bracelet and phone were in a puddle in the alley.
(Hands the bracelet and phone to JASON.)
Do you own or have access to a pistol?

JASON: When I get back to my unit. Can I get out of these fuckin' prison pajamas? I want to piss without a football-jock nurse checkin' me out. I want windows with no bars on'em.

LAWRENCE: Our windows don't have bars.

JASON: Those fuckin' locked screen things!

LAWRENCE: Promise to meet with me Monday.

JASON: You owe me twenty minutes. We have a pact. *Yes!* We'll fuckin' meet.

LAWRENCE: Start and end on time.

JASON: That's why I wanna meet at a bar. You wanna beer, you pay for a beer, you git a beer. Not so many fuckin' rules!

LAWRENCE: Last night you drank enough beer to endanger your life.

JASON: Now yer makin' drinkin' rules for me?

LAWRENCE: The infantry has rules.

JASON: So you don't git yer head . . . git fuckin' shot.

LAWRENCE: You started to say, "head."

JASON: Head, foot, ear, fingers.
(Bites a large chunk of banana and mumbles.)
Ddkkk.

LAWRENCE: What?

JASON: Dick! Body parts. What about, "How are you today, Jason?" Excuse me. "How are you today, Specialist Wynsky?"

LAWRENCE: How are you?

JASON: Great. Now, I ain't even got a name. Jest a fuckin' hospital number.

LAWRENCE: How are you today, Specialist Jason Paul Wynsky?

JASON: Thank you fer askin'. I'm fantastic. Gittin' the fuck out. Almost got laid last night, before I "endangered my life with beer." I'd tell ya, but I ain't layin' on yer sick sex couch.

LAWRENCE: You can discuss sex in that chair.

JASON: Tell you about my sex conquests? You'd like that, huh?

LAWRENCE: Conquests?

JASON: Shit. Nothin' happened. She passed me up fer Lucca.

LAWRENCE: I thought Lucca was dead in the eyes.

JASON: So did I. First night he rises from the dead and wham. He scores at my expense.

LAWRENCE: How did that feel?

JASON: You mean, how bad did that fuck with my manhood? Not much really. It's good seein' him up and goin'.

LAWRENCE: When you were drunk, did he hold you up?

JASON: Nah. He left before I downed my "endangerin' beers."

LAWRENCE: Who are the friends you drink with?

(Lights rise on JOSH on red-sand set. JASON turns and watches JOSH. JOSH toasts JASON with the Mason jar. JASON turns back to LAWRENCE as lights fade to black on JOSH.)

JASON: This guy Josh . . . Used to . . . I picked up a new book: *Collapse*. UCLA Professor. Jared Diamond . . . No questions about it?

LAWRENCE: You seem to superbly know my next question.

JASON: Superbly?

LAWRENCE: *(Imitates JASON.)* "Superbly? Not a neutral word, Doc."

(JASON laughs.)

LAWRENCE: "So why talk, Doc?"

JASON: I wuz gonna say that.
(Laughs more.)

LAWRENCE: *(Pause.)* And?

JASON: And?
(Pause and becomes deeply serious.)
'Cause I ain't finished talkin'.
(Long pause.)
Oh, big heavy silence. Underlined book silence.
(Pause.)
Doc? You ever see somebody die? In front'a ya?

LAWRENCE: I have.

JASON: Good. I mean, not good like—

LAWRENCE: I know what you mean.

JASON: So, you ask, "who?" And I say, "Josh." And you say, "Josh? Oh, Josh who used to hold you up when you wuz drunk." And I say . . . I say . . .
(Rapidly walks toward door.)

LAWRENCE: *(Hurries after JASON.)* Maybe we should go slower.

JASON: Slower? Not cost-efficient, Doc. Army's gonna fire ya.

LAWRENCE: We'll make time. What were good times you had with Josh? Talking about good times is . . . is like a beacon for brains to heal.

JASON: Beacon? Shit. Beacon. Uh . . . good times, good times. Well, me and Josh used to git ape-shit drunk together. Alcohol poisoning kind'a drunk. Stomachs pumped out kind'a drunk. Tryin' to forget.

LAWRENCE: Forget?

JASON: Fuckin' childhoods.

LAWRENCE: Josh sat in principals' offices, too?

JASON: No, no, Doc. Josh wuz good. Always tried to please everybody. Rich parents. Texas ranch. Driveway fulla cars. But his parents wuz always drunk at Texas oil, or cattle, some kind'a rich parties. Left Josh with his nanny. Mexican nanny, Lucinda. She wuz old, but he called her by her first name, Lucinda.

LAWRENCE: You know a lot about him.

JASON: Blood brothers. Josh never got laid 'til me and him went out. Outside'a Kabul. Bagram Airfield. Course, probably wouldn't a happened if I hadn't paid fer her. Josh's whore.

(Lights rise on JOSH on red-sand set and fade on office.)

JASON: *(Walks to JOSH and hands him a coffee mug.)* This coffee'll help, light weight. Drink it.

59

(JASON spills coffee on JOSH'S watch.)

JOSH: Shit! You got coffee all over my watch!

JASON: What? Yer fuckin' rich parents give you a eight-thousand-dollar Rolex Submariner and it ain't coffee-proof? My little hundred-dollar G-shock is."

JOSH: My watch is coffee-proof, asshole, but now I gotta pull off the pain-in-the-ass cover and dry it out, fuck head. You really paid fer my Russian whore? You ain't got fuckin' money fer chew tobacco.

JASON: You wuz too pussy to ask the Desert Queen fer a massage.

JOSH: I ain't remembin' nothin'.

JASON: I can't believe I blew my hard-earned pay on yer dumb ass.

JOSH: Hold on. I'm rememberin'.

JASON: You better.

JOSH: Little pink-and-orange-stitched flowers on a pillowcase.

JASON: You fuckin' remember a pillowcase?

JOSH: Little stitched pink and—

JASON: You shoved yer dick into a Russian whore and you remember pink flowers.

JOSH: Little stitched pink and . . . That's it. Fuck!

(Lights return to normal office setting as JASON returns to office.)

JASON: "Little stitched," all he fuckin' got out of it. Well, except the crabs. Blamed me. Made him hate me. Not really.

LAWRENCE: Not really being what you saw on his face? Heard in his voice?

JASON: Good times. Bagram over there. Back here Fort Bragg. Well, off-base, *Fayettenam* good times.

LAWRENCE: They still call Fayetteville, "Fayettenam?" Hmm. And then you two ended up in Iraq together?

JASON: Not Iraq.

LAWRENCE: I meant Afghanistan.

JASON: Thought we wuz gonna take this slow.

LAWRENCE: Good. Control when you want to move slower.

JASON: That's a trick to make me go faster, huh? Yer books teach you to do that? Or you always in a hurry? Push yer kids to graduate early, move out, marry, lay their lives on the line?

LAWRENCE: Did Josh's parents push him?

JASON: Did what?

LAWRENCE: Did Josh's parents push him to complete—

JASON: I heard what you said. I jest don't see how you got there from what I said. Reckless question. Yes, they pushed hard. Didn't care he had math'n readin' disabilities. Shoved him through school. Made him sign up to *learn discipline*. He was sufferin' awful. But his nanny?

LAWRENCE: Lucinda.

JASON: She wuz calm, acceptin'. Josh loves that Mexican woman. She writes him most every day. Mails care packages. Cake in a jar. His mother writes once a month. His father? Never. Sometimes in the mountains? The desert mountains?

(Lights rise on JOSH in red sand reading a letter as fade on office. Sounds of helicopters in background.)

JASON: *(Walks to JOSH.)* What's Lucinda say?

JOSH: "Yer mom and Sonia flew Sonia's jet to Chicago to buy new dresses." Blah, blah, blah. "Yer daddy met with some geologist man to search fer oil on George Hartley's old farm." I'll skip down . . . "Tell Jason it warms my heart to know you ain't alone with all that danger."

JASON: *(Grabs letter.)* "And I hope to meet him and T Rex when they come to Texas." You wrote her 'bout T Rex? Shit, Josh.

JOSH: Lucinda don't tell nobody what I write.
(Pause.)
No one writes you, huh Wynsky?

(Return to normal office lighting.)

JASON: *(Moves back to office.)* You know what she done? She writes me and T Rex same as Josh. Almost every day . . . Can we stop, please sir? I'll come back Monday. No drinkin'. I'll be exactly on time.

LAWRENCE: I'll owe you twelve minutes.

JASON: Wise-ass. Thank you, sir. Can I leave the hospital, sir? I can't stay here all weekend.

LAWRENCE: I gotta warn you about Dr. Jaynes. She is tough. I'll put in a good word for you.

(JASON nods with gratitude and walks to door.)

LAWRENCE: Before you go, where is T Rex?

JASON: I reckon somewhere outside'a Dallas. Buried in a field near some little Texas church.
(Exits.)

CHARLES: *(Stands in doorway.)* Gwynie called her friend Lisa. Lisa's our new chair for the ethics committee.

LAWRENCE: Fuck.

CHARLES: What do ya say we grab a beer away from this damn place?

LAWRENCE: This is so wrong.

CHARLES: Clyde's. Like old times.

(The lights go down to black.)

10. BAR SCENE

Sound of soft bar music and crowd noises. LAWRENCE and CHARLES drink from beer in mugs at a high table with high stools. There are also four empty mugs on the table.

LAWRENCE: I brought James here once. We sat at this table. Maybe that one. He was torn between Gwyneth's wish for him to marry Megan—or any girl I suppose—and his wish to go for the Special Forces.

CHARLES: Fire or frying pan. My second year at the Citadel, I told Barbara I couldn't stand by with all that was going down in Vietnam.

LAWRENCE: And she waited for your mean ass.

CHARLES: Dead set on a man in uniform. While I was overseas she dated a few other . . . Well, we don't talk about that.

LAWRENCE: Gwyneth blames James' death on me. Because after med school, I re-enlisted.

CHARLES: Let someone else see this kid . . . She told Lisa there's unhealthy counter-transference between you and this soldier. Plus, left-over Vietnam issues.

LAWRENCE: We all have fuckin' issues. What if my issues help this boy?

CHARLES: What if your issues send him off the deep end?

LAWRENCE: The iron is hot. I know his mind's games. When and how he hides from truth. Moments like this vaporize.

CHARLES: We'll keep it simple. Hold him over the weekend.

LAWRENCE: You'll shut him down! We sent him to war. Damaged his brain. Broke his spirit. He has hope, Charlie, I've seen it. Steal his hope, and you kill him.

CHARLES: You insult the rest of us acting like only you can help soldiers. Did you ever consider you have a blind spot for war trauma? You never talk about Vietnam, what the NVA did to us.

LAWRENCE: I don't have *kills* to brag about.
(Pause.)
I didn't mean that. Sorry.

CHARLES: You know . . . there are nights I wake smelling rotten-egg mortar powder. Singed flesh and fresh blood smells.

LAWRENCE: After forty years.

CHARLES: Know what I see over and over?

LAWRENCE: Let's don't go down this path.

CHARLES: Endless blasted tree stumps.

LAWRENCE: Tree stumps.

CHARLES: May fifteenth. The hill you and I almost died on, you holding your guts in your hands.

LAWRENCE: Three feet of guts.

CHARLES: Took a hit to the balls, too.

LAWRENCE: You're not going to fuckin' shut up, are you? I forget when you drink, you son of a bitch, you start in. Yeah, that asshole zipperhead blew off my left testicle.

CHARLES: Always wondered, how's that prosthetic ball work for you?

LAWRENCE: It jingles.

CHARLES: Jingles?

LAWRENCE: Just leave it at, "It jingles."

CHARLES: I asked. Well, I was the one that fuckin' NVA in the bunker took down first. Every day it rains, my fucked-up foot remembers him.

LAWRENCE: I should head home.

CHARLES: When I saw him blast you with his grease gun, the way he ripped your middle apart, I was sure that was it.

LAWRENCE: You saw him? . . . Damn. Glad I blacked out.

CHARLES: You didn't black out. You were blabbing crazy talk when that Marine picked you up.

LAWRENCE: *You* dragged me to the chopper. That's how you got your shiny medal.

CHARLES: A Marine carried you, you fuckin' idiot. Moses.

LAWRENCE: Moses carried me? . . . Then what?

CHARLES: Uh . . . Chopper lifted off, I guess . . . Medevac to Vandergrift . . . Barbara'll be expecting me. I'll take this one.
(Tosses money on table.)

(The lights go down to black.)

11. LAWRENCE AND GWYNETH'S BEDROOM AT NIGHT

GWYNETH is reading in bed as LAWRENCE flosses.

GWYNETH: Your silent treatment never works . . . Are you going to tell me what Charlie said?

LAWRENCE: *(Pause.)* They're holding my patient for the weekend. Starting Monday, Charlie will supervise me like I am some inexperienced, grade-grubbing medical student. He's an administrator, clueless how to conduct therapy.

GWYNETH: Charlie will assure everything is safe.

LAWRENCE: What is it you imagine I will do? Leave behind my passion for therapy? Every afternoon scrub down *Peacemaker's* decks? In a few months, you and I will adjust to James' death. I won't recover from how you strategically destroyed this young man. He glimpsed hope.

GWYNETH: At least I'm not working overtime to bring back James by turning young soldiers into best friends.

LAWRENCE: No. You go about life like James is going to jog through our kitchen door any moment, toss his sweaty T-shirt onto his chair.

GWYNETH: I'll sleep in the guest room.
(Exits.)

LAWRENCE: *(Yells.)* Thank you for that.
(He sits on the bed, lost in deep thought.)

(The lights go down to black.)

12. LAWRENCE'S OFFICE

LAWRENCE picks up the book <u>Collapse</u> from the edge of the stage, sits, and reads. He does not look up when CHARLES enters.

CHARLES: *(Looks at book.) Collapse.* Never heard of it.
 (Sits in the chair by the couch, remaining in nervous, awkward silence.)

LAWRENCE: *(Long pause as reads.)* When was the last time you supervised someone?

CHARLES: Just observing. Simple. I would not dare supervise.

LAWRENCE: Hmm.

CHARLES: They released your specialist Saturday. "Remarkable, model behaviors." That's what they charted. Fuckin' snowed the weekend staff.

LAWRENCE: Hmm.

CHARLES: Did you know Saturday night he hopped a flight down to Texas? He won't show. A waste of our time.
 (Pulls glasses from case, puts them on, and looks at watch.)

LAWRENCE: Please tell me, you didn't just put on reading glasses to look at your thirty-thousand-dollar watch.

CHARLES: You keep your damn office too fuckin' dim.

LAWRENCE: And to think you were our best sniper . . . God, we're getting old.
 (Pause.)
 I dreamed about Moses.

CHARLES: In Vietnam?

LAWRENCE: When I lost my helmet.

CHARLES: The blast blew it off your head. You screamed like a baby for it.

LAWRENCE: He put his own helmet on my head.

CHARLES: Carried you in his arms like a cradled child.

LAWRENCE: I stared at his two necklaces: a 550-cord with a triangular Buddha and a chain with a silver St. Christopher medal.

CHARLES: Covering all bases.

LAWRENCE: They rubbed together. Back and forth. I kept whispering, "Thank you Moses."

CHARLES: You wouldn't stop thanking him.

(JASON enters in full combat uniform, wearing sunglasses and carrying the book, On Killing, under his arm. He stands at attention. LAWRENCE pauses to take in JASON in full uniform and then stands.)

JASON: Two minutes early, sir. Let's call it even. No owed minutes. I'll be on time. End on time. Your and my rule, sir.

LAWRENCE: Your and my rule. Jason, let me introduce you to Colonel Scott. Colonel Scott will observe us.

CHARLES: Ignore that I am here. Go about your session as you would any session, son.

(JASON places sunglasses and book under his chair.)

LAWRENCE: *(Reads from checklist.)* Any suicidal thoughts?

JASON: No, sir.

LAWRENCE: Any drinking?

JASON: No, sir.

LAWRENCE: Urges to drink?

JASON: No, sir.

LAWRENCE: Do you feel we are progressing?

JASON: I don't like this. No disrespect, Colonel Scott.

CHARLES: No disrespect taken, Specialist.

JASON: Nice watch, sir. Rolex GMT Master. Are you reading any good books these days, sir? Colonel Scott, sir? Books? Fiction? Non-fiction?

CHARLES: I'm only here to observe you while—

LAWRENCE: For gosh sakes, Charlie, tell him the damn name of a book you're reading.

CHARLES: Oh, uh, well, I read the new *DSM Five.* Lists psychiatric diagnoses.

JASON: Pretty grippin'?

CHARLES: Why don't you two pick up where you left off?

JASON: Do you mind if I ask Colonel Scott, sir, do you have a couch in your office, sir?

CHARLES: A couch? No. I do not have a couch, son. Proceed.

JASON: No couch. I see . . . Where we left off . . . My jerk-off fantasies. You were right, sir. It's better to not fantasize about Sasha since she is an evil, ball-destroyin' bitch. Am I out of line, Colonel, sir?

CHARLES: Carry on, Specialist.

JASON: Yes, sir. So, I fantasize about Marta, Rosa, Heather, Stephanie, sweet, luscious soldiers. That time I used Cool Whip and got a rash? I had it checked out. Not cancer.

LAWRENCE: I understand you flew down to Texas.

JASON: Yes, sir. Last night jerkin' off I remembered bein' fifteen and hookin' up with two fourteen-year-old girls. Sonya sittin' on my face while Lisa palmed me off.

(CHARLES stands, requiring JASON and LAWRENCE to pop up.)

CHARLES: I hope you two will excuse me. Meeting you, Specialist? Interesting.

JASON: An honor to meet you, sir. It is wonderful the military provides people like me with places where we can discover truth. Grow into the men we are destined to become.

CHARLES: What a crock of bullshit. Don't think for a minute I don't see what's going on. Your two's conspiracy signifies an unusually strong alliance. I am not *"clueless how to conduct therapy."*

LAWRENCE: She told you?

CHARLES: She told Barbara; Barbara told me. Specialist Wynsky? Is this man helping you?

JASON: *(Stares at floor.)* Yes, sir.

CHARLES: When you address me, Specialist, you stand at attention and you look me squarely in the eye. Is this man helping you?

JASON: *(Obeys.)* Yes, sir! He is savin' my life. *Sir*!

CHARLES: *(Pause.)* Carry on, soldiers.
(Exits.)

JASON: *(Takes moment to shift to seriousness.)* When you go home, all this stuff, sex talk, nightmares . . . don't bother you none?

LAWRENCE: You worry your words will harm me—

JASON: Don't! No bounced-back-at-me answers.

LAWRENCE: I think about what people tell me. Sometimes at home. It's the way I know how to help people. It's the way I like to help people.

JASON: I know I'm a pain in the ass, but I appreciate straight talk more than you know.

LAWRENCE: You keep being nice to me like this and I'll, I'll go . . .

JASON: Go crazy?
(Laughs wildly. His laughter slowly subsides.)

LAWRENCE: *(Moment of silence.)* So, is that Josh's dog tag on your wrist? . . . In Texas, you visited Josh's grave.

JASON: *(Nods and is silent a moment.)* Doc? Do you believe in God? Angels and devils? All that shit?

LAWRENCE: It feels like there's something out there. Good forces. Bad forces—

JASON: I know God's out there on account'a I hate him. People say, "Oh, God's testin' us." Not me. God punishes me. I don't know what I done wrong. Maybe buyin' a whore for Josh. That was wrong. One time? I took five dollars outta Big Mama's purse. Took Rosie Metz out fer a hot dog and a Mountain Dew. We both got diarrhea. *(Pause.)*
You ever hear the song, "Hush Little Baby" and junk about mockingbirds and diamond rings?

LAWRENCE: I know the song.

JASON: One day we wuz way out in the Registan Desert. Oil splattered outta our Humvee. Melted my boot.

(Lights rise on red-sand set as lights dim on office set. JASON walks to the sand, sits atop his sleeping bag, and rubs his foot.)

JOSH: *(Drunk, shuffles to JASON.)* Hey, buddy. Why ain't you racked out?

JASON: Fuckin' foot's on fire.

JOSH: Let me see. Arkansas bandaged that? Damn good dressin'. Layin' on this cold night red sand'll cool yer foot.

JASON: Red sand ain't helpin' shit . . . Josh? You ever git nightmares?

JOSH: Shit yeah. They kick my ass.

73

JASON: Santiago said he don't. Said war makes him feel strong. Closer to his family. Closer to God.

JOSH: I met some'a them boys. Don't know I believe'em.

JASON: Well . . . I can't sleep.

JOSH: *(Pause to study JASON.)* You know what helped me growin' up, when I couldn't sleep?

JASON: Nope.

JOSH: Lucinda sang me to sleep.

JASON: Lucinda ain't here singin' now, is she? If she wuz, she'd wake up the fuckin' Taliban.

JOSH: Taliban ain't hearin' nothin'.

JASON: Them jerks would hear.

JOSH: Shit. They're huddled up tryin' to keep warm. Nursery-rhyme song worked every time.

JASON: You are fuckin' goofy.

(Sound of distant explosion.)

JOSH: Song about mockingbirds and diamond rings.

JASON: Shit. I ain't never seen no real diamond ring.

JOSH: Shut the fuck up and listen. When my parents wuz drunk, yellin', throwin' shit at each other, Lucinda's song put me right to sleep.
(Sings.)
"Hush little baby don't say—"

JASON: Josh! We're two grown soldiers. Taliban camps all around us and yer gonna fuckin' sing me a baby nursery rhyme song?

JOSH: Shhh. Lay still now.

(JASON lies on top of sleeping bag.)

JOSH: *(Quietly sings.)* "Hush little baby, don't say a word. Mama's gonna buy you a mockingbird."

(Sound of another explosion.)

JOSH: *(Sings.)* "And if that mockingbird don't sing, Mama's gonna buy you a diamond ring."

(Return to normal office lighting as JASON moves to office.)

LAWRENCE: And?

JASON: And? . . . I fall asleep . . . Only night's sleep I'd had in months. God took that. So yeah. I hate him. Where were the angels? All the fuckin', singin' angels. Not there. Not later.
(Removes dog-tag bracelet and clutches it.)
Doc? Were you ever an altar boy?

LAWRENCE: Altar boy? No. I was not.

JASON: I think mostly poor kids are altar boys. Course you may not even be Catholic. None'a my business. I wuz one. Altar boy. And you know what? I prayed hard. Every night. By myself. Prayed to God to have a friend. Sound stupid? A little kid prayin' to have a friend?

LAWRENCE: No.

JASON: Well, sounds stupid to me. But I did. Almost every
. . . Almost every . . .
(Stands, places bracelet on desk, quietly exits.)

*(LAWRENCE walks to desk, stares at bracelet. He packs
his briefcase and walks toward the door, but is blocked
when CHARLES enters.)*

LAWRENCE: Charles. I used to look forward to your visits.

CHARLES: I bragged to Lisa and Gwynie about your
alliance with Specialist Wynsky.

LAWRENCE: You did? That's good. We had a breakthrough.

CHARLES: The ethics committee wants you to prescribe
medications for nightmares. Refer him for pastoral
guidance. You are limited to one more session.
Understood?

LAWRENCE: Cost efficient . . . I'll refer him to someone I
trust in the private sector.

CHARLES: The Army won't pay for that.

LAWRENCE: Not a problem.

CHARLES: If you personally pay for this boy's private—

LAWRENCE: There will be nothing in my notes. You can
retire in a couple of years, Charlie, a completely
uncomplicated send-off.

CHARLES: Go fuck yourself, too.
(Walks toward door.)

LAWRENCE: Clyde's later this week?

CHARLES: Don't even pretend it's not your turn to buy.

LAWRENCE: Wait. I'll walk out with you . . . Charlie? Is there something about Specialist Wynsky that resembles James?

CHARLES: I remember James in footy rabbit pajamas, terrorizing his little sister. Later in his Michael Jordan jersey. Not very good with a basketball.

LAWRENCE: James thought he was good.

CHARLES: No. You thought he was good.

(They both exit.)

GWYNETH: *(After a moment, enters, carrying a letter and already talking.)* Lawrence? Jacqueline needs for you to sign her . . . Oh.
(Walks to Lawrence's desk, finds paper, and stands while writing a note.)

JASON: *(Enters.)* Oh . . . Sorry. I left my glasses and book.

(GWYNETH resumes writing her note. JASON walks to chair, kneels, picks up sunglasses, stands, and stares at GWYNETH.)

GWYNETH: *(Looks up.)* Do I know you?

JASON: No ma'am.

GWYNETH: *(Stares for a lengthy moment.)* You move like my son. Stand like him.
(Pause.)
This is wrong. I shouldn't . . . I'm sorry.
(She tears up the note and rushes out.)

JASON: *(Walks to the photo frame, picks it up, studies it, and returns it. He walks to shelf and picks up the*

77

display box with the folded flag inside. He reads the plaque on the box.)
"Specialist James Frederick Caplan . . .   November 7, 2009."
(He holds the flag box against his chest.)
They're crawlin' up outta the sand . . . Comin' fer me.

(The lights go down to black.)

13. LAWRENCE AND GWYNETH'S KITCHEN - DAY

JACQUELINE, sitting on a kitchen stool, chats into her mobile phone as she simultaneously checks her laptop's messages. GWYNETH enters with a small gourmet-style bag of groceries and eavesdrops.

JACQUELINE: I passed my physical with flying colors. So? It's my life. Not theirs."
(She sees GWYNETH.)
Gotta go. Nathan's supposed to call. Later.
(Ends call.)

GWYNETH: I didn't expect a visit from you today. How is Nathan?

JACQUELINE: Fine, I guess.

GWYNETH: I hope you aren't going out with him. He has tattoos.

JACQUELINE: We don't date. We study together. Besides, he has a . . . significant other.

GWYNETH: Nathan can judge what is significant?

JACQUELINE: Mom? Did you really just say that?

GWYNETH: I heard you say you had a physical.

JACQUELINE: You were eavesdropping.

GWYNETH: Anything wrong where we need to be concerned?

JACQUELINE: I signed up for the Air Force.

GWYNETH: You what?

(JACQUELINE walks away.)

GWYNETH: Stop right there!

JACQUELINE: It's my life.

GWYNETH: This is because of James.

JACQUELINE: Do you realize how insulting that is? You never value my capacity to make decisions! Never!

GWYNETH: I do trust your decision-making.

JACQUELINE: No, you don't! You trusted James. Never me.

GWYNETH: James didn't keep secrets from me.

JACQUELINE: *(Valley-Girl cadence.)* Oh my God.

GWYNETH: Exactly what does that mean, young lady?

JACQUELINE: You knew nothing about him.

GWYNETH: How dare you.

JACQUELINE: Oh. So, for example . . . He told you he was gay?

GWYNETH: What?

JACQUELINE: What I thought.

GWYNETH: How can you even suggest a thing like that?

JACQUELINE: Seriously?

GWYNETH: I'm his mother. I would know.

JACQUELINE: Oh, really?

GWYNETH: What? He told you? Said that exact word to you? Gay?

JACQUELINE: Gay! When he was eleven, and I was nine. You've never been able to see who we are because you're too busy wishing we were someone else. They must not have taught anything about delusions in your psych program, and they sure as hell didn't teach about denial. And to set the record straight? Signing up for the Air Force isn't for James. It's for me.
(Exits.)

(GWYNETH slides to the floor, sitting paralyzed.)

(The lights go down to black.)

14. LAWRENCE AND GWYNETH'S KITCHEN - DAY

GWYNETH zips her roller suitcase, looks in her purse, and pulls out her keys.

LAWRENCE: *(Off stage.)* Thanks for the packing boxes! . . . Where are you?

GWYNETH: In the kitchen.

LAWRENCE: *(Enters.)* We achieved a major breakthrough. *(Sees suitcase.)*
Where are you going?

GWYNETH: To visit Sarah. She requires sisterly advice.

LAWRENCE: Overnight?

GWYNETH: She needs to talk about her divorce. I need to talk about our children.

LAWRENCE: What the—?

GWYNETH: You should feel proud. *Your* daughter signed up for the Air Force.

LAWRENCE: What? She has two semesters left. I won't permit it.

GWYNETH: She's twenty. Following your glorious footsteps.

LAWRENCE: She never hinted that she—

GWYNETH: In med school, you promised me that Vietnam was the end of everything military. You lied to me. I ended up with all my family fighting in wars. Dying in wars.

LAWRENCE: That's unfair.

GWYNETH: Killing in wars. Living with ghosts. You think only you soldiers live with ghosts? You're wrong. We live with those ghosts, too.

LAWRENCE: I never encouraged our children toward the military and you know it.

GWYNETH: Every time you spotted a soldier, you fell over backwards. Your friends' stories, your father's stories.

LAWRENCE: I never told them war stories.

GWYNETH: Exactly. And your silence was deafening.
(Rolls her suitcase to the door. She comes to a standstill and speaks with her back to Lawrence, concealing her pain.)
Did you know James was gay?

LAWRENCE: Uh . . . Yes. Yes I did . . . Did you?

GWYNETH: I suspected, but . . . Did he talk about it?

LAWRENCE: Just before he left for Afghanistan. He asked me not to tell you.

GWYNETH: Oh . . . I see . . . I can't imagine how difficult . . . being gay, being in the Army.

LAWRENCE: He said it was . . . difficult.

GWYNETH: You allowed him to go.

LAWRENCE: He insisted.

GWYNETH: *(Directly confronts LAWRENCE.)* If I—his mother—had known my son was gay, you can bet your sweet ass I never would have allowed him to go to Afghanistan.

(Sound of door chime. GWYNETH opens door.)

BARBARA: *(Standing outside, holding a pie.)* Hope you don't mind I came to the back door. Did I come at a bad time? I brought you a grasshopper pie.

(The lights go down to black.)

15. LAWRENCE AND GWYNETH'S KITCHEN – TWO HOURS LATER

GWYNETH and BARBARA are sitting at the bar, extremely intoxicated.

GWYNETH: I have to eat something, or I'm gonna have a whopping hangover.

BARBARA: Eat my grasshopper pie.

GWYNETH: Does it have grasshoppers in it?

BARBARA: Gracious no. Like the drink—

GWYNETH: I was joking—

BARBARA: Crème de menthe, crème de cacao, Oreo crust.

GWYNETH: Yuck, I mean . . . Nice. What's the occasion?

BARBARA: Oh, yeah. Charlie said Lawrence was having a tough spell. Don't tell him I told you. Charlie swore me to secret.

(GWYNETH crosses her heart and holds up two fingers.)

BARBARA: What was that?

GWYNETH: Swearing . . . I think.

BARBARA: Oh . . . What did you ask me?

GWYNETH: Why you brought me a bug pie.

BARBARA: For uh . . . for uh nightmares . . . Vietnam. Lawrence's nightmares. Charlie has'em, too. Never talks about'em, of course.

GWYNETH: Idiots. They think we don't notice.

BARBARA: So obvious.

GWYNETH: Did I tell you James is gay?

BARBARA: Two glasses ago. Or four.

GWYNETH: He told Lawrence. Told his sister. Not me. No. Not me. I'm his mother. A fucking psychiatrist. I would never, never, never allow him to . . . to uh—

BARBARA: Go.

GWYNETH: Go! Go to Afghanistan. I'll never, never, never forgive him. Lawrence. How the fuck do you—Excuse me—How do you put up with all this military crap?

BARBARA: I told you.

GWYNETH: Tell me again.

BARBARA: Well, Dad was a teenager—

GWYNETH: Uh huh.

BARBARA: In World War Two—

GWYNETH: World Wars, that's right, that's right, World Wars. You did tell me.

BARBARA: Dachau. Survived the Death Train.

GWYNETH: You never told me about trains. You should write a book.

BARBARA: American soldiers rescued him. He never said much about it.

GWYNETH: They never do.

BARBARA: My sister and I have our lives because they rescued him. US soldiers rescued him. My dad.

GWYNETH: No one rescued James.
(Pause.)
Especially not me.
(Pause and then screams.)
My baby boy killed himself!
(Cries.)

(BARBARA tightly hugs GWYNETH as they both sob, until BARBARA grabs a paper towel and dries her tears and then GWYNETH'S tears.)

BARBARA: Remember you told me you liked my bush?

GWYNETH: Liked your what?

BARBARA: My April Snow Rhododendron bush.

GWYNETH: Yes. Rhodo- . . . Yes.

BARBARA: I have one for you in the back of my car. A small one. But it'll grow—

GWYNETH: Thanks, but—

BARBARA: Before you say you can't garden worth a hoot—

GWYNETH: I can't—

BARBARA: I discussed it with Charlie. And we agreed with me, I mean, *he* agreed with me . . . We'll check uh . . . soil, water . . . garden stuff. You know . . . You don't have to lift a finger.

GWYNETH: That's so nice!

BARBARA: It'll be well loved.

GWYNETH: That is the sweetest thing anyone has ever given me. A snow . . . a snow thing.

BARBARA: *(Tries to articulate but slurs.)* April . . . uh, Snow . . . Rhodo- . . . dendron.

GWYNETH: That thing. That is so sweet.
(Leans over and hugs BARBARA and then abruptly sits up.)
Oh, my!

BARBARA: What's wrong?

GWYNETH: I've got to apologize to Jacqueline. Oh my gosh! I owe her the world's biggest apology. I've got to call her.
(Enters phone number.)

BARBARA: Don't! Not in *this* condition!

GWYNETH: Oh! You're right . . . Okay . . . I think I'm ready for grasshoppers.

(The lights go down to black.)

16. LAWRENCE'S OFFICE

LAWRENCE places his book Collapse into a box and then spots the book On Killing under Jason's chair and retrieves it.

LAWRENCE: "Dave Grossman. *On Killing.*" Hmm.
   (Skims to inside chapter.)
   "Killing at Mid- and Hand-Grenade Range: You Can Never Be Sure It Was You." Whoa.

JASON: *(Enters, agitated and pacing.)* You know how I know God's out there? Cause I'm a devil. Not *the* devil. *A* devil. There's lots'a devils out there. I'm one of'em.

(LAWRENCE moves near the panic button.)

JASON: You ever make a pact with anybody? Like when you wuz a kid? Swear on it, spit on it? I never did. Not 'til Josh come along.

LAWRENCE: What was your pact with Josh?

JASON: Cowboy story shit. "Don't let'em take us alive."

LAWRENCE: The Taliban?

JASON: "Boogieban," Josh called'em. Said, "Boogieban drag you off. Skin you alive."

LAWRENCE: Boogieban.

JASON: I know you see where this is goin'. So why talk about it?

LAWRENCE: When you read your books? And the words move you.

JASON: Words are my enemies, racin' 'round up here when all I want is a little sleep.

LAWRENCE: Do you ever tell people what you read?

JASON: Miss Buckland. Josh.

LAWRENCE: Sharing helps people to feel better.

JASON: I'll lose it!

LAWRENCE: You won't lose it. You just won't be alone with it anymore.

JASON: Doc? Are my chances decent?

LAWRENCE: I hope so.

JASON: Hope so? . . . Hope so. Guess I better be nicer to God.
(Picks up folded flag and holds it near his chest.)
Any more tricks from them underlined books?
(Returns flag to shelf.)

LAWRENCE: What if . . . What if I try to tell *you*, your and Josh's story?

JASON: You'll massacre it.
(Lies on the couch.)
Tell me my own story.
(Slaps the couch.)
Earn your pay, Colonel!

LAWRENCE: That's steep, Specialist Wynsky.

JASON: I'm bettin' it all on you, sir.

LAWRENCE: Let's see . . . You and Josh are patrolling. It's a blue-sky day.

JASON: It's always sunny in Tarok Kolache.

LAWRENCE: Hmm. Smells of pomegranate orchards. Kandahar's Arghandab River Valley. The two of you.

JASON: Four of us, sir. We wuz sent down an alley.

LAWRENCE: Josh, Bags, and?

JASON: Phillip. We call him, "Arkansas."

LAWRENCE: Josh, Bags, and Arkansas.

(Lights change from office to village lighting with one overhead spotlight on LAWRENCE. A backdrop or image of Afghanistan houses appears.)

LAWRENCE: *(Dazed, remembering.)* Four of you, down that alley. Some villagers. Mostly men. Fewer than usual women and children. Not a good sign.

JASON: *(Dazed, remembering.)* Then no women and children.

LAWRENCE: Men become sparse until that alley is almost empty.

JASON: Then not even one village man in sight.

LAWRENCE: Very bad sign.

JASON: Bad sign, Bags. No men.

(JOSH and JASON walk among village houses. JASON talks to LAWRENCE as if still in the office. LAWRENCE remains in the spotlight, talking as if JASON were still on the couch. Sound of machine-gun burst.)

JASON: PKs.

LAWRENCE: Russian machine guns.

JASON: Bags and Arkansas are down.

LAWRENCE: And Josh?

(Spotlight on LAWRENCE goes to black. More machine-gun blasts and JOSH falls.)

JASON: *(Crawls to JOSH.)* Fuck! Yer leg's blown up. We gotta take cover, buddy. Ten feet that way. That open door.
(Drags JOSH and then holds him in his arms. Both become quiet and listen.)

JOSH: *(Quietly coughs into his hand and calmly examines it.)* Blood . . . My chest.

(Sound of village men yelling outside, "Derdzem, derdzem . . . Mur!")

JOSH: "Mur." That's Pashto fer "dead."

JASON: Shit! Bags and Arkansas. I left Bags and Arkansas in the alley.
(Stands and peeks through window curtains.)
I fuckin' left'em.

JOSH: You only had time to pick one. You picked me.

(JASON flinches twice to the sound of two distinctly spaced rifle shots. A Taliban man yells, "Mur." Sound of burst of machine-gun fire and glass shattering followed by silence. JASON dives to JOSH and they are quiet again.)

JASON: My knee! Shit. I can't feel my foot.

JOSH: *(Calmly sticks hand in jacket, feels chest, retrieves bloody hand. Resigns.)* Jace? Tell T Rex I ain't got no chance. Sorry, buddy.

JASON: *You* tell him. We're gittin' out.
(Tries to lift JOSH but cannot with his injured knee.)
Josh? Listen.

JOSH: My watch. Busted. Blood all over it.

JASON: Listen! Me and you'll crawl out.

(Sound of door of neighboring house being kicked in, followed by machine-gun fire.)

JOSH: The Boogieban are shootin' up houses. They's comin' fer us. A few seconds and those psychos'll be at our door.

JASON: Crawl!

JOSH: They're gonna take me.

JASON: They can't have you.

JOSH: They're gonna skin me.

JASON: I won't let'em.

JOSH: Look at me.

JASON: No.

JOSH: Git outta here, Wynsky. That's an order, soldier.

JASON: I won't leave you, Josh.

JOSH: No time left.

JASON: No.

JOSH: *(Takes the pistol from his belt and holds it out for JASON.)* One shot . . . Me and you got a pact.

(JASON hesitates. JOSH nods. JASON accepts pistol and stands behind JOSH, who struggles up onto his knees and turns his back to JASON.)

JASON: Wait.
(He retrieves T Rex from his pocket and hands it over JOSH'S shoulder.)
Take T Rex. Put'im in yer pocket.

(JOSH nods and places T Rex into his pocket.)

JASON: Take care'a him fer me.

(Spotlights rise on LAWRENCE and on JASON and JOSH. Other lights go to black.)

LAWRENCE: *(Stands at parade rest, looking at JASON, whispers.)* Just . . . one . . . shot.

JASON: *(Turns to LAWRENCE.)* He's my friend.

LAWRENCE: It's what Josh asked you to do.

(JASON holds the pistol execution style to the back of JOSH'S head. JASON pauses, drops the pistol and hobbles to LAWRENCE, dragging his injured left leg.)

(Return to normal office lighting.)

(JASON hugs LAWRENCE. LAWRENCE hesitates to hug, holding out his hands for a moment. He finally wraps JASON in a hug. JASON lunges further into grasping LAWRENCE. LAWRENCE helps JASON to the couch, pulls a white handkerchief from his pocket, and pours water

*onto it. He cautiously hands the handkerchief to JASON,
backs into the middle of the room, and crouches in a
low, safe, non-threatening position.)*

LAWRENCE: How did you get out?

JASON: A small closet. I piled clothes over me. I heard
them drag Josh into the alley. I climbed out back.
Outside, me and Lucca wuz blasted by an explosion.
They found Josh two days later. Boogieban burned him.

LAWRENCE: I'm sorry, son . . . I know I just hauled you
through hell, but I read in your record that you received
a Bronze Star with V device. For actions taken in
Khosrow. Can you tell me about that?

JASON: Jest . . . gittin' in position to shoot over the wall,
lookin' up at the hill where they wuz firin' hard down on
us . . . later celebratin' we had took out two'a their PKs.

LAWRENCE: Any more memories from that event?"

JASON: No, sir. Try hard as I can, I can't remember more,
sir.

LAWRENCE: This will be difficult, but I want to record us,
part of your evaluation. Okay with you?

(JASON nods.)

LAWRENCE: *(Gets recorder and cautiously sets it near
JASON.)* Specialist Jason Paul Wynsky? Do you
understand and agree for me to record your statements
as we complete your psychiatric evaluation?

JASON: *(Softly.)* Yes, sir.

LAWRENCE: Just a bit louder for the—

JASON: Yes, sir!

LAWRENCE: You were referred by Captain Kendall for nightmares. Did we discuss those nightmares in detail?

(JASON nods.)

LAWRENCE: Answer with words, son.

JASON: Yes, sir.

LAWRENCE: On the day of February 5th, you and Specialist Josh, Joshua?

JASON: McCrae.

LAWRENCE: Specialist Joshua McCrae came under attack patrolling in Tarok Kolache.

JASON: Yes, sir.

LAWRENCE: You were caught in crossfire, lost two men. After Specialist McCrae was fatally wounded, the two of you held up in a village house.

JASON: Yes, sir.

LAWRENCE: Did Specialist Joshua McCrae say anything to you? . . . Specialist Wynsky? Did Specialist McCrae say anything to you?

JASON: Jest . . .
(Clears throat.)
Jest . . . "Tell T Rex . . ."

LAWRENCE: Rounds hit the house you and Specialist McCrae held. Bullets penetrated your left knee.

JASON: Yes, sir.

LAWRENCE: Specialist Wynsky, where did the fatal round strike Specialist McCrae? . . . Son? Can you show me?

(JASON holds his index finger high behind his own head like a gun for several seconds. He quickly rams his finger into the base of his own skull, execution style.)

LAWRENCE: Was it possible to tell if the fatal round that killed Specialist McCrae came from hostile fire or from friendly fire?

(JASON nods, holds his hand out in front of himself, points by hitting his own chest with his out-stretched thumb.)

(The office lights dim and LAWRENCE walks into a bright spotlight.)

LAWRENCE: What does the Army want me to do? What would other military psychiatrists do? What does this human being in this room at that this moment need me to do? What choice can I live with for the rest of my life? *(Pause.)*
The Army trained me to be a double agent, to help soldiers, but more importantly, champion strict allegiance to the command. I am to be compassionate, but my duty, my ultimate goal is to get soldiers—the military's expensive resources—back up and fighting as quickly as possible. Quicker than possible. If I—or any other military psychiatrist—continues working with Jason, there will be investigations, hearings, a trial. Some will accuse Jason of murdering Josh. Others will accuse Jason of committing the most unforgiveable sin, wasting the Army's expensive resource: another soldier. *(Pause.)*
There are moments in therapy when twin souls are born. Intimate moments. Those moments nourish me, enable me to move from soldier to soldier. Addictive

moments of awe. Two beings peering upon sacred stories with identical understanding, identical thoughts, identical emotions. I am a mirror for Jason, and Jason for me. We lie in bullet-splattered mud beside one another. We are alive and our lives, God damn it, are worthwhile!
(He returns to JASON as office lights abruptly rise.)
So! Specialist McCrae was killed in the line of fire.

(JASON is stunned.)

LAWRENCE: *(Motions to JASON to say yes.)* Killed in the line of fire.

JASON: *(Hesitant.)* Yes, sir.

LAWRENCE: A bit louder.

JASON: *(Angry.)* Yes, sir!

LAWRENCE: Later, the enemy broke into the house, dragged Specialist McCrae's body into the alley, and burned his body.

JASON: Yes, sir.

LAWRENCE: Are these events the contents of your nightmares?

JASON: Yes, sir.

LAWRENCE: Every night?

JASON: Yes, sir.

LAWRENCE: Thank you, Specialist.
(Paces as dictates.)
I am entering Specialist Jason Paul Wynsky's diagnosis as posttraumatic stress dis . . . diagnosis as

98

posttraumatic stress, the result of witnessing deaths of three friends by enemy fire. I further recommend that Specialist Wynsky is not fit to return to duty at this moment and that treatment for PTSD should commence immediately. I shall make those arrangements. Lieutenant Colonel Lawrence Caplan, 16 hundred hours, 37 minutes, Tuesday, 27 April 2010.

JASON: That was a lie! Sir!
(Throws down handkerchief.)

LAWRENCE: Jason? . . . Look at me . . . Please? . . . War is about lies. Lies start wars. Lies end wars. Lies help us to move on, put devils behind us.

JASON: I *am* the devil!

LAWRENCE: If I had been Josh, I would want *you* by my side . . . Your courage . . . Your love.

JASON: I hid! I listened to'em shoot more bullets into'im. Drag him outta that house. I got to crawl out! He didn't! *(He cries.)*

LAWRENCE: *(Sits close enough to JASON to almost be touching.)* You will continue to have nightmares. In time, harsh nightmares will soften, not occur as often. *(Speaks from personal, painful war experiences.)* Our nightmares never go away, but there are days, nights, when we are free of them. *(Works to regain composure.)* I arranged for a private therapist. As you talk, kindness and the truth will connect to your nightmares. One day, there will be so much kindness and truth, devils and angels will all mix together. When that happens, you will sleep.

JASON: I want you to be my therapist.

LAWRENCE: I don't work for my patients. I work for the command. They'd rip you apart. No.

JASON: Please, sir?

LAWRENCE: No.

JASON: But you're my friend.

LAWRENCE: I am your friend.

JASON: Will I be able to go back?

LAWRENCE: Go back? You want to go back. Yes, of course you do. Aim for that.

JASON: Colonel Caplan? Doctor, sir? . . . I want you to know . . . I met your son. We had lunch together in the mess hall at Bennin'. Like you, he was nice. I can't picture him or you ever bein' mean to nobody. He wuz somebody to be proud of, sir.

LAWRENCE: Thank you for that.

JASON: Can I lay down, sir? On your couch? I won't stay long.
(Picks up handkerchief, politely holds it out.)

(LAWRENCE accepts it.)

JASON: Jest a moment, sir.

LAWRENCE: Sure, soldier.

JASON: I don't want to be alone right now, sir

LAWRENCE: I won't leave you, son. I am standing guard.

JASON: Thank you, sir. Thank you, Colonel.

(Lies on the couch and immediately falls asleep.)

(The lights shift to black except one overhead bright white spot just outside the office perimeter. Sound of a helicopter landing. LAWRENCE walks into spot, looks up, and shades his eyes. He slowly lowers his gaze as if observing the helicopter land. Sound of helicopter fades to silence.)

LAWRENCE: Moses.
(Pulls out his phone and calls.)

(A second overhead bright white spot rises, illuminating CHARLES.)

CHARLES: *(Answers phone.)* Colonel Scott.

LAWRENCE: Moses lifted me into that chopper. I looked into his eyes, took in his big smile.

CHARLES: He was happy to get you into that chopper.

LAWRENCE: He should have been wearing his helmet. I handed it to him. To put back on his head when . . . when . . .

CHARLES: When the back of his head exploded. Splattered over us . . . Every day, I see you live enough life for two people. We are our fathers. We don't tell our stories. We don't tell ourselves.

(Bright spots fade to black as two soft spots rise: one on the desk and one on the couch where JASON is asleep.)

LAWRENCE: *(Walks to desk and picks up the bracelet.)* Jason? . . . Jason?
(Kneels by couch and places bracelet beside JASON.)
Specialist Jason Paul Wynsky . . . Thank you.

(Spotlight on couch fades to black.)

LAWRENCE: *(Walks to desk, changes tape in the recorder, and dictates.)* Fallen soldiers decompose in hallowed fields, beneath mud mounds, beneath desert dunes. Small bits transform into dust and gas, mingle with specks of iron, wash into rivers and oceans. Into space . . . We spring from that. We return to that. For some reason, somewhere in between, we are granted moments. Small-as-can-be moments.
(Studies family photo frame.)

(A soft spotlight rises downstage as the desk spotlight goes to black. LAWRENCE walks into the downstage spotlight and calls on cell phone. A second spotlight rises on GWYNETH as she answers phone.)

LAWRENCE: Gwynie?

GWYNETH: You missed dinner. I had asked Jacqueline to join us.

LAWRENCE: I'm sorry. We ran over. It was our . . . last— I'll try to leave soon. Can you wait there?

GWYNETH: Uh . . . I could. I guess.

LAWRENCE: Is Jacqs still there?

GWYNETH: Upstairs changing. We were about to go out for dessert.

LAWRENCE: Please wait. I have a story I want to come home and tell you. I just wish James . . .
(Cries softly.)
Wish James could hear it.

GWYNETH: You're scaring me.

LAWRENCE: *(Regains composure.)* No, no, it's not . . . It's, it's about Vietnam.

GWYNETH: Oh, Lawrence, not tonight. It's been a long—

LAWRENCE: Please? This is important to me.

GWYNETH: Okay, okay. I'll . . . We'll be here.

LAWRENCE: Thank you.
  (Pause.)
When I was wounded, Vietnam, there was a Marine. I never told you about him. You would have loved him. The three of you would have loved him.   He had this big . . . warm smile. His name . . . was Moses.

(LAWRENCE breaks down crying, as does GWYNETH.)

(BLACKOUT.)

About the Author

A native of the South, DC Fidler has combined a career in academic psychiatry and cultural psychiatry with a lifetime of playwriting, acting, directing, composing music, and teaching creative writing and the dramatic arts.

He studied theatre, writing, chemistry, medicine, and psychiatry at the University of North Carolina at Chapel Hill, where he served on the faculty. He later served on the faculty at West Virginia University, teaching cultural psychiatry, clinical psychiatry, and acting.

A licensed psychiatrist, DC Fidler has lived and worked with the Alutiiq tribe in Akhiok, Alaska, the Al Moqbali Bedouin tribe near Sohar, Oman, the Kalkadoon Aboriginal Tribe in the outback of Queensland, Australia, and the Te Tau Ihu Maori Tribes on the South Island of New Zealand.

He began his acting career in outdoor dramas, summer stock theatre, and local films and television at age ten. He has written scripts and composed music for over fifty medical educational videos at UNC-CH and WVU. He has written seventeen plays that have been produced in various community theatres and universities across North Carolina, Virginia, and West Virginia, as well as St. Louis, Sacramento, San Diego, Los Angeles, Boston, Chicago, and New York City.

He consulted and appeared in educational productions for HBO, ABC, and PBS and performed in numerous stage plays including: *Hope is the Thing with Feathers, Night of January 16th, Thieves' Carnival, Blood Wedding, Our Town, A Life in the Theatre,* and *Fool for Love.*

Presently, he is a scriptwriter, film director, and medical consultant for educational films using professional actors to demonstrate mental health issues. In addition, he is an active member of the Dramatists Guild of America and the Charlotte Writers' Club.

Fidler previously chaired the Video Committee for the American Psychiatric Association and served as President of the Association for Academic Psychiatry. In 2003, he was inducted as a Fellow of the Royal College of Physicians of Ireland. He serves on the Arts and Humanities Committee for the Group for the Advancement of Psychiatry where he is co-producing a video series on the History of Psychiatry, and using the arts to teach people about mental health.

He is author of the textbook, *Psychiatry for Actors: Using Psychiatric Principles to Build Characters,* and author of the novel, *Boogieban.*

Musicals by DC Fidler
- Pied Piper
- Healer Man
- Medicine Show

Plays by DC Fidler
- Voices in the Woods
- Guilt by Association (With RJ Casey)
- Three Diaries
- Master William Bowlinggreen and Company
- Shiraz
- The Anniversary of Miss Nanette Pringle
- School Children Hiding Under Desks
- Grams
- Camp Uni
- Boogieban (Two-Actor Version)
- Boogieban (Seven-Actor Version)
- Ahulaqs
- Elk and Wolf (With Travis Teffner)
- Santee Delta (With Travis Teffner)
- Celtic Crossing
- Stone Touchin'
- Daugherty Park Merry-Go-Round
- La Dynastie
- Gyges Solution

Short Plays by DC Fidler
- Persons
- Cruise
- Mobile to Where
- Oman Truce
- Second Amendment
- The Greek God Club
- Four X
- Microscopic Misconceptions
- Drone Guns
- Moon Bugs (WithTravis Teffner)